Praise for *Loving Che:*

"*Loving Che* displays the same radar for the telling emotional detail that Ms. Menéndez's impressive [*In Cuba I Was a German Shepherd*] did. . . . [*Loving Che*] appears to take as its model the intense, lyrical voice of Marguerite Duras's best-selling 1985 novel *The Lover*. . . . Expands the talented Ms. Menéndez's fictional terrain."
                              —Michiko Kakutani, *The New York Times*

"Splendid . . . What makes *Loving Che* truly memorable is Menéndez's intense imagining of Teresa's Havana. . . . Che's photographs add bright images of youth and nostalgia, snapshots of a lost world."
                              —Richard Wallace, *The Seattle Times*

"[Menéndez] brings alive the spirit of Guevara and the heart of the revolution in a novel that aches with longing, loss, and lust-driven love. . . . Menéndez pays tribute to her people and her culture in *Loving Che*."
                              —Carol Memmott, *USA Today*

"A beautiful and quite possible reinvention of history."
                              —Alan Cheuse, NPR

"Inventive and hypnotic . . . [*Loving Che* is] Menéndez's deliciously mischievous take on the exile's endless capacity to blur history—both personal and political—into myth. . . . A tart fable about history and identity that is equal parts detective story, travelogue, and fever dream."
                              —Mark Rozzo, *Los Angeles Times Book Review*

"The pain and loneliness of exile . . . permeates this poetic, fragmentary first novel by Ana Menéndez. . . . Conjoin[s] love and history and politics into a powerful mélange. One of the strengths of this book is that while its backdrop is one of the most politically charged events since World War II, Menéndez's focus is on a much more intimate drama; she uses the revolution because it illuminates her theme of separation. . . . Menéndez's literary sensibility also reveals itself in strongly, often beautifully poetic prose."

—Timothy Peters, *San Francisco Chronicle*

"A moving commentary on the Cuban diaspora in Miami . . . . *Loving Che* is at its best when it subtly details the Cuban migration. . . . Menéndez does an excellent job conveying the longing some Cubans have for their homeland."

—Andrea Ahles, *Star-Telegram*

"[A] poised and elegant first novel . . . It is breathtakingly convincing . . . its mood is perfect."

—*The Irish Tatler* (Dublin)

"The power and beauty of the framing narrative . . . suggests that Menéndez may be up to something much smarter and more ambitious than another overtly familiar tale of doomed lovers in exotic circumstances. . . . The writing is gorgeous, and the portrayal of Havana under the revolution as one of romantic decay is . . . sharply rendered. . . . A finely tuned modernist novel in the tradition of Italo Calvino or Vladimir Nabokov."

—Chauncey Mabe, *San Antonio Express-News*

"A refreshingly different take on a subject and country about which few people are neutral."

—Nickie Witham, *City Life* (UK)

"*Loving Che* deftly captures the fluid sense of identity that accompanied the now mythic early days of Cuba's revolution. . . . Menéndez is at her best when depicting [the] social detail, revealing what life is like for many Cubans today. She captures Cuba's potential, its desperation and decay, and also its dark humor." —Ruth Lopez, *The New York Times Book Review*

"[*Loving Che*] puts [Menéndez] in the company of other Latino writers such as Junot Díaz and Sandra Cisneros. . . . Capture[s] the spirit of revolution and unrest in Havana in the late fifties and early sixties." —*Vanity Fair*

"[Menéndez's] details are so palpable, her narrative so believable, and her research so deeply imbedded in her story . . . that readers could easily be hoodwinked into thinking they were reading a memoir instead of a novel. . . . In addition to being an exuberant and poetic look at loss and memory, *Loving Che* is also . . . an enticingly erotic reimagining of the passionate first days of the Cuban Revolution." —Chris Watson, *The Santa Cruz Sentinel*

"[Menéndez] has written an evocative, if fleeting, love letter to a salt-of-the-earth guerrilla lover, a vanished world and the eternal ruins of memory." —Anderson Tepper, *Time Out*

"The story, flicking back and forth in time as one would flick through a photo album, paints a powerful portrait of Cuba, and dwells on the fine line between the shadows of imaginings and the solidity of reality." —Philippa Logan, *The Oxford Times*

"[Menéndez] vividly renders a wounded yet optimistic Havana, wracked with both violence and exhilaration in the early years of the revolution. . . . She deftly weaves many well-known details from Che's life into the figure of a dream lover." —Katie Millbauer, *Seattle Weekly*

LOVING
CHE

Also by Ana Menéndez

In Cuba I Was a German Shepherd

LOVING CHE

CHE

Ana Menéndez

Grove Press / New York

The author and publisher gratefully acknowledge the following for the right to reprint material
in the book: pp. 9, 14, 120, 121: "Letter on the Road" by Pablo Neruda, Translated by
Donald D. Walsh, from THE CAPTAIN'S VERSES © 1972 by Pablo Neruda and Donald D.
Walsh. Reprinted by permission of New Directions Publishing Corp.; p. 13: 1968, "Cuban
artist's installation" © Fred Mayer/MAGNUM PHOTOS; p. 50: 1958, "National tribute to
Che Guevara" © CORBIS SYGMA; p. 55: 1958, "National tribute to Che Guevara" ©
CORBIS SYGMA; p. 83: 1958, "National tribute to Che Guevara" © CORBIS SYGMA; p. 87:
"Ernesto Che Guevara" © CORBIS SYGMA; p. 100: 1960 "Ernesto Che Guevara" © Andrew
Saint-George/MAGNUM PHOTOS; p.123: "Ernesto Che Guevara" © CORBIS SYGMA;
p.126: 1967, "Ernesto Che Guevara's body" © Hulton-Deutsch Collection/CORBIS; p.156:
"1963 Ernesto Che Guevara" © Rene Burri/MAGNUM PHOTOS; p. 163: "El Encanto"
courtesy of Don Julio, Asociacion de Antiguos Empleados de El Encanto, Inc.; p. 226:
"Ernesto Che Guevara" © CORBIS SYGMA.

Published simultaneously in Canada
Printed in the United States of America

FIRST GROVE PRESS EDITION

Library of Congress Cataloging-in-Publication Data

Menéndez, Ana, 1970–
    Loving Che/Ana Menéndez.
    p. cm.
    ISBN 0-8021-4174-9 (pbk.)
    1. Cuban American women—Fiction.   2. Guevara, Ernesto, 1928–1967—Fiction.
3. Illegitimate children—Fiction.   4. Mothers and daughters—Fiction. 5. Americans—
Cuba—Fiction   6. Revolutionaries—Fiction.   7. Women—Cuba—Fiction.
8. Birthmothers—Fiction.   9. Miami (Fla.)—Fiction.   10. Cuba—Fiction.   I. Title.

PS3563.E514L68 2004
813'.6—dc22   2003060714

Grove Press
an imprint of Grove/Atlantic, Inc.
841 Broadway
New York, NY 10003

05 06 07 08 09   10 9 8 7 6 5 4 3 2 1

For Dex

Whenever I travel, I like to spend the last day of my journey in the old part of town, lingering for hours in junk stores whose dusty shelves, no matter where in the world they may be, always seem to be piled high with old magazines and books and yellowed photographs. I am a nervous flier, and this excavating into other people's memories never fails to soothe my fears on the eve of departure. The photographs of strangers, especially, have always brought me a gentle peace, and over the years I have amassed a large collection of serious and formal-looking people caught in the camera's moment. Many of the subjects of these old photographs, I've come to notice, carry a grave shadow about their mouths, as if they were already resisting the assertion that these images might represent their true selves. Some nights, when the blue hour is falling, I will take out one of my photographs and imagine that the stranger caught there is a half-forgotten old aunt, or a great-grandmother who smoked cigarettes from a long silver holder. But I know that I'm playing a game with history. For all my imaginings, these images will remain individual mysteries, numbed and forever silenced by the years between us.

* * *

Ana Menéndez

Some years ago, I became interested in the photographs that exiles had taken out of Cuba. It was common, I found, to frame the photos or place them in albums, to be taken out now and again in the company of friends. I thought I would construct a traveling exhibition of these photographs, and was even able to secure funding for the project. But I ran into delays and other problems. Many families, I was dismayed to learn, would not give up their photographs, not even for a few days. And when, in a purely innocent gesture, I agreed to accept the photographs of exiles who had fled Batista, my political motivations were put in question and the entire project fell apart.

Disillusioned, I abandoned my plans and came to interpret this fetish for the past as another of the destructive traits of the Cuban. Miami seemed to me in those years to be living in reverse. They named even their stores after the ones they had lost; and the rabid radio stations carried the same names as the ones they had listened to in Cuba, as if they were the slightly crazed sons of a once prominent family. This endless pining for the past seemed to me a kind of madness; everyone living in an asylum, exiled from the living, and no one daring to say it plainly.

I wonder now if this backward looking of the exile—the Cuban one in particular, so hysterical and easy to caricature—could be an antidote to a new and more terrible kind of madness. The exile, whatever the circumstances of his leaving, may wake up one night, as a traveler in an unfamiliar room, and wonder where it is he may set down his feet, in what direction lies the door by which he entered. Perhaps this trauma of

separation—beginning from our very birth—is the normal se-
quence of things and to detach oneself, to learn to move freely
about the world without longings or inventions, takes years of
patient learning; and even then we may turn one day and find
the years hollowing a dark canyon beneath us.

Of my own origins, I know little. I was raised by my grandfather in a western suburb of Miami in a small house that was
almost indistinguishable from the other houses on the street.
Every morning he walked me to school and every afternoon
we returned home together. When he spoke it was to point
out a particular type of tree that he wanted me to know about,
or the name of a flower that was growing in someone's garden. In the evenings, he would sit in his bare yellow chair and
read for hours in silence. After, when I had gone to bed, my
grandfather would turn on the shortwave radio he kept inside
the cupboard. Every night, I drifted to sleep listening to stations coming in and out of tune, the peculiar whine punctu-
ated now and then by a low-hummed bulletin in Spanish or
the scratching notes of a danzón played out over distances I
could not yet fathom.

In my grandfather's house there was no television set, no
magazines, no photographs, only books and the quiet turning
of pages. Of my parents, as of most things, he spoke little. I
grew up with the understanding that my father had been in
prison, and had died there, and that in her grief my mother
had sent me away. If I asked my grandfather any questions of

her when I was a child, I have little memory of it. Perhaps I sensed already that she had been part of some great disappointment, that she was one of the many things of the past that it was best not to speak about. It is true, also, that for the years of my childhood, my grandfather comprised the whole of the world I knew. Yet somehow, in spite of these buried sorrows, he had managed to give me an uneventful, even pleasant childhood; and what I remember most now are the ordinary markings of growing up: splashing in a plastic pool with the neighborhood kids, my Catholic school uniform and the comfort of being part of a group that agreed on important things. Perhaps my grandfather, with his private memories of turmoil, had set out to give me a bland and ordinary life; or perhaps that is the life that comes to those who have stopped struggling to make sense of things.

The time came, however, when my grandfather's silence about my mother no longer satisfied me. As a girl I had already begun to sense a void behind me, and as I grew older I became more and more preoccupied with the blank space where my mother should have been. As I passed into my adolescence, I spent more and more time thinking about her, and in each imagining she grew more beautiful, more exciting, more different from the woman I myself was becoming. The easy respect, the love, I had shared with my grandfather slowly came to be overlaid with frustration and distrust. The more questions I had for him, the more he seemed to retreat into the quiet of his books. When I asked him once why he didn't have one photograph of my mother that he could show me, he responded, simply, that she had never given him one.

Our disagreements always managed to skirt the edges of our loneliness, however, and I found I could never leave him. Even after I enrolled at the university I would return home every Saturday to sit with him for lunch. Sometimes, when the weather was good, he retreated to the porch after the meal to smoke a cigar. One day, instead of doing the dishes first as was my custom, I decided to join him right away. I sat beside him and after a moment decided to help myself to a cigar as well. My grandfather's eyes widened ever so slightly for a moment, but he remained silent. I sat still, looking out into the yard. After a few minutes, he put out his cigar and I did the same. A bird called and then was gone. Something rustled in the grass. It had rained that morning and the breeze carried now the moist earth smell that reminds us we step on living ground.

I began by telling him about my classes. He asked me a few questions about what I was reading. He listened and then said, For literature there was no one like the Russians, not even Shakespeare. Only the Russians, my grandfather said, understood that a man cannot change his nature. I looked at him, but he didn't turn to me. So one shouldn't even try, I said. My throat burned, and the discomfort of it perhaps lent my voice an annoyance I hadn't meant. My grandfather shrugged. Just accept, I continued. With this he turned to me and said, very softly, You have no right to be angry at me. At who then? I said, trying to keep my voice equally low. My grandfather didn't respond. I don't understand, I said slowly, how you could have gone these years without trying to get in touch with her. I paused. If only for me. My grandfather didn't move and I continued, rushing now to fill up the pauses: I don't understand how you have not one photograph, not one letter, not one document. For all I know I have been raised in a lie—what's to keep me from thinking you didn't kidnap me, or even that you're not really my grandfather? With this last, I knew I had pushed too hard, and fell silent. After a long while, my grandfather said, You want documents, photographs. This is truth to you? I didn't answer. I heard my grandfather shift in his chair, and then we were quiet. When I turned to him, I saw that his hand shook where he had brought it to his cheek.

After a long while, my grandfather said, We had a lemon tree in the courtyard of our house. A small tree—we grew it in a pot. But it gave good fruit. When she was a little girl, your mother used to pick the lemons and eat them one by one in little bites. My grandfather paused. Even then she was so beautiful that she did what she wanted. The effort would twist her little face, but still she would bite into it. My grandfather looked at me. His eyes turned down, but he managed a smile that deepened the lines in his face. Then he leaned back in his chair and let out a sigh. This rain will be good for the ferns, he said. After a minute, I said, Why? I said it so quietly that he might not have heard me. He sat for a little while and then, pressing his hands against the wooden arms of his chair, he lifted himself up. The sliding glass door behind me opened and shut.

The shadows lengthened and then spread. I became aware gradually of music coming from the shortwave, and I recognized the sad voice of Toña la Negra. When the song was over, another came on, and then another, all of them carried on a whisper. I had scarcely moved. For some years, I had been aware in myself of a strange detachment, an aimlessness. I could sit for hours and do nothing, feel nothing. Now I heard every small rustle in the grass, every labored ant-step.

I sat out on the porch until it was almost dark. The sliding door opened again behind me and I turned. In his hands, my grandfather carried a worn piece of yellow paper.

It had been her idea, he said after he had settled into his chair. I didn't want to take you away from her. But she insisted. She said she wanted you out of the country. My grandfather lit the small candle between us. He picked up the note again and when he sat back, his giant shadow materialized behind him. For years, I tried to contact her. Every May, on her birthday, I wrote her a letter. If I have no letters to show you now it's only because she never responded. Some years ago, my grandfather continued after a moment, I asked a friend who was traveling to Havana to take her a package. My grandfather turned to me. Some drawings you had made, and yes, a school photograph of you. But when he got there, he found the house filled with five different families. Teresa had vanished.

My grandfather and I sat. In the silence, a far-off cricket sang, followed by the sound of the breeze rolling like a fire. She herself had arranged things, he continued. In six months, she would join us. My grandfather sighed and fingered one of the edges of the paper in his hands. In the candlelight he seemed older than ever, shadows exaggerating his bony fingers, highlighting the fragile fabric of the skin over his knuckles. When I applied to leave the country, he continued, the government took my house. I still had to wait for our visa. I had no choice but to move in with her, into the house I had given her. At night, I could hear you crying. Some nights, you cried all night long without stopping. I don't know if she left you where you were, or if you cried in her arms; I never left my room. It was December, he said. The day we were to leave, she brought you to me, wrapped in several blankets. She laid you on the bed and you didn't move, wrapped up like a little moth, big eyes looking out over the room, resting now and then on an object; it was almost as if you were taking inventory. She gave me a bag of your things—some clothes, bottles, and the brown bear that you lost one year at the fair. Remember how you'd cried? And I told you it was nothing, that we would get you another one. But you can imagine what I, too, felt.

My grandfather opened the paper in his hands. I had removed your blankets somewhere along the way. But it wasn't until we arrived in Miami that I noticed that your mother had pinned a note to your sweater. I threw it away immediately, without reading it. And then that night, I took it out of the trash. I was never going to show it to you. What is the use of keeping these things? My grandfather smoothed the paper out on his lap and handed it to me with the same shaking hand I had noticed earlier.

I held the note in my hands for a long while. Finally I bent down to read by the yellow light of the candle.

Farewell, but you will be
with me, you will go within
a drop of blood circulating in my veins

I read the lines several times. And then I refolded the paper and sat looking out into the darkened yard until my grandfather rose, saying that the damp night would do us harm.

A few months later, I dropped out of college and began to travel. One windy December day, I drove up the coast to Sebastian Inlet. I stopped at a small hotel and became its only guest. The first morning, I took a magazine to the beach and sat out all day, wrapped in a blanket, listening to the waves. When the sun began to set, a flock of seagulls rose against the deepening sky like a hundred evening stars and I sat and watched them until night fell.

As the months and then years passed, I traveled farther and wider, my desire to keep moving always outpacing my small terror of planes, my fear of leaving. I was in India when I got word that my grandfather had died. It took me three days to get back to Miami, by which time I had missed the funeral. I stayed with friends for a few days before returning to my grandfather's house to sort through his things. The first night alone in the house, I was unable to fight the feeling that at any minute he would turn a corner and wave in the shy manner he had. The house was filled with a new silence that seemed to muffle even my attempt to mourn. Unable to sleep, I sat up all night in his chair, reading one of his books on the growing and care of ferns.

Shortly after, I made my first trip to Cuba. When I landed and saw the capital by the red light of sunset, I knew I had returned to find my mother. I took a room at the Habana Libre and spent days walking my grandfather's old neighborhood— knocking on doors, waving to women in their balconies, reciting to anyone who might listen the name of my mother and the three lines that were my only connection to where I had come from. I made several more trips, each as unsuccessful as the last. And though I met many people and passed out my address to anyone I thought might have known my parents, I waited in vain for word. Eventually, I stopped traveling to Havana, the trips leaving me more and more exhausted, not only from the uncertainty but from the sadness that I came to understand more clearly with each visit. Havana, so lovely at first glance, was really a city of dashed hopes, and everywhere I walked I was reminded that all in life tends to decay and destruction.

I settled in a small beach town north of Miami, supporting myself by writing short articles about the places I visited. I found that it was possible to write about a city without having to talk to anyone. And I even came to believe that this was a more honest way to work, capturing the purity of place without the complications that human beings tend to introduce.

I traveled by myself and returned home alone and after a while decided that the unease that had settled over me would fade with time. One afternoon, when I had arrived at my house after weeks away, I found a package waiting for me. I would have let it remain unopened for another day had I not noticed that it had been forwarded from an old address in Miami Beach where I had lived for a time during my trips to Cuba.

The package, which had been postmarked in Spain without a return, was secured very carefully, and it was clear that someone had taken great care to protect its contents. The box itself was flat and rectangular and wrapped in a thick tape. Even so, its edges were soft and dark from wear. I turned the box over several times, trying to find where the strip of tape began. I thought I had found it on the back, but when I tried to put my nail under it, I saw that it was only a crease in the wrapping. After some time of this turning and turning of the box, I stood and went for a knife and gave the tape a quick cut. When I pulled, the tape peeled off cleanly and quickly, almost as if it had been of one piece. Beneath the tape, thin ropes wrapped around the box, indenting the edges. I tried to pull them off but finally these, too, I had to cut. I held the bare box in my hands now, the surface gone fuzzy where the tape had pulled away. It was not very heavy for its size. I shook it. Nothing rattled, nothing shifted. I moved to open it, but my fingers trembled on the box. I had to stop then and close my eyes, and after I had regained my peace, I peeled at one of the sides with my fingernail until the tab came loose.

The papers and photographs that spilled out smelled of dark drawers and dusty rooms. Some fell apart when I touched them. Some of the letters were written in such a small hand that it was as if the writer were whispering secrets into my ear. I hoped, at first, that by arranging the notes and recollections in some sort of order, I might be able to make sense of them. But on each rereading I found myself drawn deeper and deeper, until I feared I might lose myself among the pages, might drown in a drop of my own blood.

LOVING CHE

Falsos me parecieron mis primeros esfuerzos.
Y ahora solo quedan estas rajas de memoria,
escritas sobre banderas de viento. . . .

One day, when I had already grown old with the revolution, a woman came to my door and asked to see the lady of the house. It was June and my sixty-fifth summer in Havana. I had the blinds drawn against the heat, but the windows were opened behind them and I could hear Beatrice telling the woman no one was home. She didn't leave and instead called up in her young woman's voice, saying she only wanted a quick visit. Then, as if she knew I was listening behind the blinds, she recited in a deep and serious voice: *Farewell, but you will be with me* . . . I felt the years heavy on my chest and finished the lines softly to myself: *I found you after the storm, the rain washed the air, and in the water, your sweet feet gleamed like fishes.* I sat in the afternoon heat and waited for her footsteps to fade. I heard Beatrice come up the stairs and I heard her pause behind me and then move on.

Later, when the sun had gone down, the woman returned. Beatrice was below in the kitchen peeling tomatoes for the evening meal. I waited a few minutes, listening for sounds on the street, and then walked out to the balcony myself. The young woman turned her face up and I saw, even by the yellow light of the lamps, that her dark hair was pulled back low and the ends curled around her neck in a style that was familiar to me. She was young and slender and I can say—without regret or false modesty, as old age has long since stripped me of these conventions—that she reminded me of myself at the same age. Her Spanish had the rounded edges and swallowed vowels of Cuba, but she wore slim black pants and angular shoes, so that I knew she was not from here. She told me her name and said she was looking for a woman who had given up her baby daughter years before. I told her she had the wrong house; that I was nobody. She asked if she might come up and talk. I said I was sorry that she had been misled to my house. She stood there on the street looking up at me for a long moment. I imagined her trying to make out my face in the darkness, recognizing the years on it. Then all at once she apologized, hands open in front of her. She waved, and still looking up at me began to walk down toward the sea. I watched her until I could no longer make out her figure in the dusk.

That night, the old wind blew and the windows rattled in their frames. I could smell the coming rain. Beatrice lit a yellow candle in the hallway and I lay in bed, watching shadows flicker beneath the door.

I remembered another night when the wind sang with ghosts. He lay beside me in the dark, listening. Memory, he'd said, is a way of reviving the past, the dead.

When you live for a long time in one place you begin to confuse your life with the city; its avenues and landmarks come to stand for your memories until you become the tourist of your own past, viewing a younger self with the fascination of someone just passing through. For so many, the past has gone soft with distance, so that when they talk of a building that used to be beautiful or an avenue that once burst with yellow flowers in March, they are really talking about a self they wish to have been. I am afraid, if I tell the story now after all these years of silence, that I will be confused for one of those dreaming tourists who point out only the graceful and vital, who are happy to deal with the surface of things.

As a child, I had been one with weather. When we went down to the farm on the weekends, and the nights without moon were so black that you could scarcely make out your fingers in the dark, I used to lie awake, battered this way and that with the sound of the wind. If there was a storm coming, I could feel it miles away, smell it; and often I would wake the family, my parents and all the cousins, with my howling. This is when I began to wonder if perhaps the outer world was no more real than our imagination and all its thrashings but a mirror of our own thoughts. And I wonder now if our recorded history isn't like this, if our idea of history isn't another way of saying an idea of ourselves. First comes childhood, the innocence of times gone by, then the trauma of awakening to pleasure and pain, and then the expulsion, the revolution: all our private fears and desires cloaked in the great story of man. Behind us lies our beginning, ahead of us only oblivion. Because it is the old who look back, sometimes with fear and sometimes with joy. The young are all revolutionaries, struggling toward the future, convinced that just over the rim of sky—There; there!—lie the happiest times. But both the old and the young indulge in longing. And the older I get now, the more that longing for the past seems the only true course. Why idealize the future, where only death awaits? How much lovelier to think on the past when we were young and untested and our beginning lay behind us like a forgotten dream.

When I was a girl, it seemed to me Havana was full of beautiful women. They had their dresses made in the shiny window shops, where the seamstresses wore white gloves so as to not soil the material from Europe. The salons were filled with women reinvesting in themselves—massaging thick cream into their heels, curling their hair to emphasize pretty slanted eyes, a plump cheek. Women ate their dreams and bloomed like orchids in the rain.

My two sisters knew, too, how to rest their heads on their hands so the line of their long necks formed the symbol for longing. They had a way of moving their gold hair off their shoulders, slowly, as if in doing so, they had discovered a way to prolong the day. The men came to sing to them after dinner, when they sat on the porch to take the evening breeze, and their girl laughter took on the color of sunset.

My own hair was thick and dark and I wore it short against my neck. In the evenings when the others sat on the porch, I climbed to the roof and watched the sun go down over the rooftops, letting my hair dry in the breeze, watching the horizon where the sky came every night to be swallowed by the ocean.

I was smaller and darker than my sisters, with a boy's skinny hips. The men did not sing songs to my window at night. In the afternoons, the suitors who came for my sisters forgot my name at the door. But I saw how the men leaned back from their wives at the little restaurant by the cathedral, the way their eyes darkened to match my own. A young girl and already knowing that silence held the heavier balance of truth.

My mother let me roam the streets; she gave up on me long before I knew it. In the clear tropical mornings, before anyone was up, I left through the back door and went down the alleys of sleeping dogs. A different neighborhood. The rain and heat, the saltwater you could taste everywhere in Havana, got inside wood and metal. Cars rusted, foundations wasted. It took everything to keep the street-side faces of the house smooth and neat. Every year a new coat of paint, new curtains behind the windows, brass knockers taken down and soaked. The alleys were the dim backsides of so much industry. Paint peeled away with abandon and mold darkened the empty places. Where the cement had cracked, small purple flowers blossomed, as if every house held a garden prisoner within its walls. I ran through the alleys, wild for the disorder that, young as I was, shone exotic and beautiful in the light that slanted through the buildings.

I am walking in the old part of town after a storm, the cobblestones slick and shiny. I am beginning to like narrow streets, dark places. The city is my first love. I delight in the simple things: a curved cornice that catches the sun on an angle, the yellow of a billboard showing through the top windows of someone's home.

The rain runs through the grooves in the stones and the slide of tires echoes down the alleys. Laughter seeps from little rooms like sweet medicine.

At a corner, I stop to let a car pass, a black Chevrolet sequined with the reflection of street lamps. A light goes out in a room above me; a sliver of lacy curtain pulls away. The car stops and men's voices sound low and angry. I stand, pressing myself against the damp old walls. The driver opens the door and pulls a man out from the back. His face is turned and in the dark I imagine a shroud covers his head. He stands in the headlights. Another man gets out of the car. He is dressed all in white in that muddy alley, white shoes and pale straw hat collecting water on the rim, falling in tiny droplets like a veil about his face. The man goes to the shrouded figure and bends over him, speaking quietly. He walks back to the car. The laughter from small rooms. And then the pistol shot. And the man's life passes before me as if I had been the one to die: I remember breakfast that morning, looking out over the street, buttering bread, slowly stirring coffee, watching sugar dissolve. I remember his loves as my own and lean against the stone and cry for all the things I haven't finished.

The tires slick on the road, and then the rain rushing through cobblestone again.

Against the wishes of my mother, I go to the hotel to hear the old mulato play Lecuona because he always makes me cry. I pull my hair back, low on my head, and curl the ends around my neck. I wear red lipstick and the old mulato player bends his head when I lay my arm across the piano.

Every Friday, I give him a peseta and after, when the people have gone, he kisses my hand in the dark.

From certain angles, El Prado seems to run straight to the sea, as if it were a ship with a deck of flowers. The benches lie sunbathing under black iron lamps. I am almost fifteen, too old for toys and sweets, but on a bench I eat the chocolate I buy from Señor Juan, letting it soften on my tongue, begging it to last. I think of the other children still locked inside their classrooms, my sisters of the golden hair, the Almeida girls, the boys who come in the evening to call. And I with the afternoon melting around me, a patch of sky all my own through the clouds.

It is winter and the women wear brown and navy, defying the green, the flowering plants, the sky so blue the eyes hurt. It is winter, warm and bright, and the women wear hats as they walk down El Prado on the arms of their men. Broken conversations, the rustle of fabrics, women's laughter. They bend their heads so the rims of their hats cover just their eyes, highlight white rows of happy teeth.

A tall, thin man in a red hat stops in front of me and asks why I'm not in school, a pretty little thing like me in clean clothes who must have a mother and a father at home. I eat my chocolate slowly. I tell him I am orphaned. It's too late now to take it back. And I smile because I have no fears. The man stares, one eye drooping. He is thin, but his hair falls thick and shiny beneath his hat. When he turns to go, I stand and follow him. He looks back once and then rushes to the top of El Prado as if I were chasing him. The women nod at him and then giggle. Some of the men tip their hats. The thin man stands on top of a bench and claps. A small crowd gathers. Loco, Tell us a story, they call. He takes off his red hat with an exaggerated arc. He bows deeply and pretends to fall off the bench. The women laugh and the men throw coins. The man puts his hat back on his head. It lies crooked and I laugh and point. The man grows serious, puts a finger to his lips before speaking: Before the beginning, he whispers, the island was empty and the wind was without voice and the fish walked through the sand leaving footprints that lasted for years.

The man bends at the knees, pretends to tiptoe like a fish.

And then God saw this green jewel, the man says, this perfect island, and he raised a great army of angels and declared himself minister for eternity.

A woman in black clasps her hands to her chest. What a fine mimic! she says. The man next to her nods. All madmen sound like someone else, he says.

When my mother died, we laid her body in the front hall-way and my sisters hung the geraniums, whose perfume still smells to me of reproach. We kept everything as it was: the curved rosewood chair with its cool straw mat, the carved table her parents had bought in Spain. We watered the plants as she had, and at the same time of the day. When they shriveled, we kept them in their pots until the dirt cracked and sank amid the roots.

I heard voices below and I knew they'd come for me, the nuns with their black hats in the tropical sun. My mother had probably received them in her bedclothes and when they paused, I imagined they were studying her soft face, the bags of sleep beneath her eyes.

A girl her age, they said.

I stood outside my bedroom, above the stairs. My mother's voice came up slow. Without the languorous face to attach the voice to, she seemed a stranger. When the nuns left, my mother called me down. I sat at her feet. She was silent as she braided my hair. My mother was alive, almost frivolous with my sisters. But when she and I were alone, we barely talked. Sometimes I would turn and see her contemplating me and she would nod.

My mother braided my hair and I sat, my eyelids almost closing in the afternoon heat, the sound of cars below like a lullaby. After a while she stopped and I turned to look.

You have to go to school now, she said.

I tried to shake my head, but she brought her hands back to my braids and held me tight.

You're hurting me, I cried.

She undid the braids quickly, pulling, her fingers stiff and cold on my scalp. She turned me around roughly.

You are a girl and you think the world is this small. But there is a lot you don't understand, little lady. Tomorrow morning and the day after and the day after, you are going to school. I don't care what you do after, I don't care what you do before. But the nuns will see you in class. I bit my lip to keep from crying and then I bit it to keep from speaking. My mother bent to kiss my forehead, then left the room.

After I was married, I left my mother's house to my father and my sisters. Every Sunday I continued to visit. They received me on the porch where years before they had waited for their suitors. We drank coffee, talked of the events in the hills.

The last time I sat on the porch with my sisters, the years were already galloping upon us. In weeks, my oldest sister would be gone to Spain with her Galician husband. But that last afternoon was like the others. We drank and even laughed. It was one of those cool Havana afternoons, the sea air thin and fragrant. And when it was late, my sister sat at the piano and played Bach as she always had, the notes spilling onto the streets all out of context, like leaves in the wind.

One morning, I am walking through the alley. Maybe I have returned to school, the school of nuns where mirrors have been banished and the sisters bathe in white sheets that hide them from themselves.

It is hot again, yellow-green heat like liquid. The buildings stand blurred in heat against the sky. From above, the sound of pots and metal spoons, children crying. I am walking in the slender shadow of corners. The wind is still, blocked by the solid houses that have sucked the last gusts into their dark rooms, breathed the ocean into dusty corners. What reaches the alley is the exhalation, the hot detritus of a day, soiled paper and coffee grounds and soft black-skinned fruit.

A woman leans out of a window, finds me walking and leans back into shadow. A moment later, she returns with a bucket. The dirty water fans out ahead of me, splashing into black pools. A dribble slides down the side of the building. The woman shuts the window with a bang. When I come to it, the window is still shaking. The day is very bright. I walk. The heat wends inside me like a yellow illness. I want to remove my blouse where it sticks to my back, let the air lick my bare skin clean. I am soaked beneath my skirt; the sweat runs down my legs. The sky

darkens at the edges. Maybe there will be rain. I turn
onto a narrow street and cross into the next alley. Rain,
yes, and thunder. I can smell it. And then up ahead, behind an open door, movement. I stop. A dog barks. A
radio sounds. And then quiet. And above the quiet, a low
moan. They stand pressed against the wall opposite me,
a house down. They have opened the door to hide in its
shadow. The man's hand moving inside the woman's
blouse. The hand moving like wild heartbeats beneath her
blouse. And then his hand emerging, hungry, to her neck
and down, down her back, down to her waist, pressing.
He draws the flowered skirt in front of him, reaches
underneath. The woman's shoulders fall, her head tilts
back to show the white rise of her throat. Sweat darkens
the man's shirt. And then he turns his face very lightly and
his eyes meet mine, the blackest eyes beneath thick
brows. He watches me watching him. Then he blinks
slowly, once, twice. And his eyes close and I am still, heart
beating, sweat like cool stars on my skin. Other sounds
return. Children's laughter. A door slamming. I turn and
they are gone, the door shut, their wedge of private
shadow now in full sunlight, spilling like brilliant water
into the footprints in the dirt.

This is where I begin to live.

Eddy Chibás, unlucky Eddy who even now rests under an unlucky sign, is the first man I love.

Every Sunday at eight, I turn on the old mahogany radio in the study to listen to his voice. Some nights, I raise the volume until the sound trembles coming through the speakers and my sisters bang on the walls to get Eddy to be quiet. But I want his voice to last longer than these Sunday minutes mingled with the sound of dinner; I want to go on hearing it forever. His voice is hungry; it comes from beneath deep waters. Seagull's voice, voice of tongue-tied rapid railroad runners, voice of the drowned man. I don't want to see what Eddy looks like. I want to know him only by the way he says, Honor, honor, honor.

On August 15, 1951, I climb the stairs to the study. I open the heavy wooden blinds, hoping to catch a breeze, but the night is still and hot. An electric sky flashes in the distance. Tonight Eddy's voice catches on the air. A chair scrapes across a bare floor. Eddy wants sacrifice, justice; one cannot love the way he loves without pain. Eddy's beloved island, forever disappointing him. And he the faithful lover, squandering fortune and sanity in search of honor.

This is my last call, he says across the rooftops of the darkening city, past the lonely alleys, through the open windows, his voice skirting the edge of the hot night to lodge itself in the stars.

No one realized he'd shot himself—a commercial had been playing when he put the pistol to his stomach. Unlucky Eddy, Eddy the madman, Eddy who would fast for days, Eddy who held his head underwater. Eddy, my first love.

One year later, the coup, like a great shot in the dark, ended the illusion that the future was forever. The constitution of 1940 was buried without pallbearers. I watched our greatest men tear their own flesh, and I thought of Eddy, to whom death must have come like a great hunger.

This is the island Martí gave us: a green lip taunting us with its loveliness, calling us back to the black edges. Suicide is our one constant ideology; our muddy heart's single desire.

On May 28, 1953, I married Calixto de la Landre, having first fallen in love with his voice—crying, Mr. Peanut Vendor!—as I crossed the park on my way to an art class. A blue voice, I thought, with flecks of gold. And because I had picked this voice out of all the voices in the city, it seemed a mystical thing and true that I should know the man who owned it. This was the way I always knew love would come, like a burst of color in the throat.

Calixto, as I came to know, was a professor of Spanish, and he spoke with the careful diction of a man grateful for his life's work. When he objected to this or that political position, it was not out of conviction only, but out of distaste for the way it had been articulated. Over the years, I came to consider this stern defense of language evidence of a certain calcification of belief, but at the time I found his thoughts clean and unadorned and in service of the same truth that I was just then trying to discover through my painting.

My new husband busied himself with writings for scholarly journals in Spain. These writings, which I never came to understand, focused on the idea of language as a precise science that might be dissected and rebuilt in a way that aspires to heal as something out of a laboratory might. It was a rough Jungian hope, the idea that language had developed along with our deepest selves and still carried inside it our oldest wishes and fears—and just maybe the secret to our salvation. What was Calixto proposing? No one knew. And his writings were so obscure that no one ventured to guess out loud. Sometimes I suspected that he proposed the complete destruction of language as a way to progress. Other times I wondered if he wouldn't destroy everything in order to preserve the purity that had once resided somewhere in the sentence but that was now under attack by modern man, with his babble of radios and half-written newspapers. We might ponder, he wrote in a typical passage, why the Romance languages are so rich with syllables and colors, trellised with flowers and diversions so that we cannot say a plain thing even when we think it and all our endeavors become hopelessly entangled in the baroque.

Though he was much older than me, Calixto and I shared many things, including a cushioned upbringing and, appropriate to the sentiments of those times, a growing unease about it. He had long been estranged from his parents. Since my mother's death, my father and I had rarely spoken. With the years, the space between us had widened, until it seemed we could not be heard across the abyss without shouting at one another.

My father did not attend my wedding—he was traveling in Spain. But when he returned, he came by every week for coffee and a year later made us a gift of the house in El Vedado. Perhaps it was out of remorse, or perhaps, as Calixto believed, he was trying to keep me beholden to him. In any case, against my husband's wishes, I accepted the house on L Street, which, unfortunately, was around the corner from the construction site of the Havana Hilton. There was a terrible racket, of course, which perhaps my father had taken into account all along. Some days the pounding and heavy machines would shatter on deep into the night. It was then that I began to despise the Americans, with their monstrous shiny buildings, the clanging of their ceaseless industry. Constant noise has a way of slowly driving you insane. And after a few months, I decided to take a studio in a run-down fourth-floor apartment in the old city. If Calixto objected, he didn't say anything, though he never came to visit me there. The studio's light wasn't as good as the house's, but it was quiet and I could work in peace and I came to love it there.

The house had a wide porch that served to cool the inside. The floor was laid with terrazzo and the wide windows came with wooden blinds like the ones in my mother's home, all of which gave the house a feeling of coolness, so that the only air conditioner we ever needed was in the bedroom. It was built around a small central courtyard, as was the house I grew up in, and when I wasn't in the studio, I grew miniature roses there that I took now and then to the children's hospital.

Calixto began to devote more of his time to the student groups. I assumed that the parade of young men who came to the house on occasion were part of whatever movement Calixto was involved in at the time. He kept me out of most of it. But in truth, I never cared for politics. And to follow politics in Cuba in that time, you needed a purpose and concentration that I've never had. Groups came apart over obscure points and the aggrieved formed new groups—the Revolutionary Student Directorate, the 26th of July movement, the Popular Socialist Party, the Second National Front of the Escambray— each trying to outdo the other. And, my God, only a linguist could keep up with all the names.

The decade wore on and the disturbances worsened, like a summer cloud still growing to the west, not yet ready to give up its rain: a body found in the stadium, two sisters tortured and murdered, windows broken. At night, gunfire drifted through the open windows like thunder from a demented half-world. I read of a twenty-seven-year-old man who was shot to death at Los Hornos, his assassins fleeing in a green car. A thirty-five-year-old man shot to death in Chicharrones. The worker in Mabay, killed perhaps because he was related to the candidate for mayor. The man shot to death at the fence of his farm El Almiqui in Bayamo. A guajiro shot. The army blamed the rebels and the rebels blamed the army and the army blamed the rebels. . . .

I listened for the storm advancing, the fast report of raindrops on the window. We held our umbrellas up, and finally the rain came for us.

I had a good friend from school who had been walking up Twenty-third one bright March morning. Later, telling me the story, she said that the city had seemed unusually quiet. Then, out of nowhere, a black car came racing up the street, and it was some moments before my friend realized that the sounds coming from the back were gunshots. She didn't have time to see who they were shooting at. She ran to a business and started knocking on the door. But it was the noon meal and the women inside— she could see their faces—were terrified behind the locked door. The shooting went on for an eternity—these were the words my friends used as she told the story— and it was only later, after she had run home and taken a tea, that she realized she'd been shot in the calf.

I awoke earlier than usual. The house was quiet except for Beatrice's radio coming up from the back rooms. The sunlight through the window was green. The buildings were cast in its green pallor. Even the sky was green. I left through the back door. On the street, the people walked like marionettes, every move measured and false. Havana was without sound. Out past our street, I walked, round the seawall. The men in white moved their lips at the street corners, waving their dirty pictures, and not even the cars could drown out their silence. I could still hear Beatrice's radio, telling time. The hour is now. . . . The hour is now. . . .

And then, beyond the green light that fell every-where, beyond the muffled corners of the city, a crack like a tear in the sun. I ran with the others, racing to the place where the day unraveled. That delicious rush of danger like an ecstasy I could inhale. Men and women ran from buildings, spilling out over the sidewalks, into the streets, their movements fluid now, so natural. Shouting and machines cracking and still I ran. The crowd thick-ened, blood around a wound.

Someone shouted that the presidential palace had been taken. The radio station was in our hands. But the afternoon was still green with sunlight. This story goes round and round like the hands on a clock and you can pick it up anywhere. The sun still out, all the celebration tapered to a single cry. The bullets like a sudden terrifying rain. Blood that darkened on the steps. Faces crushed to the sidewalk. Around me, the crowd reversed suddenly. My knees hit the pavement and I lay there very still, my heart beating in my temples.

And then a woman's voice, slick with tears. Echeverría is dead!

José Antonio Echeverría was so gorgeously lost, even before the last bullet found him near the grand steps. What faith these beautiful men have. To storm the dictator at noon. To declare victory while drowning in puddles of steel.

After Echeverría, I lay awake in bed for two nights. I ate nothing but milk and sugar. Calixto found me one morning on the back steps, wrapped in a blanket, reciting quietly, Green, how I love you, green. Green gusts. Green limbs.

The bombs went off on street corners, in schools, outside movie theaters. Everywhere I saw the crushed faces of March 13. The shadow of a bird made me remember: I had run toward the palace with the others, all of us running. And then the pigeons in the plaza suddenly rose as one, like a black veil lifting. And then the bullets, tearing into time, opening the day into another one, letting me see the other side of things. As a girl, I had thought only love could change us so completely.

Love. Already I have used the word too often. Do you demand now that I explain myself, define what I myself never understood?

My dear daughter, I weep to see how much I have failed you. You are lovely. I could not take my eyes off of you. And I followed you down the street until you turned and were gone. The next day I traced your steps on the cobblestone over and over again, amazed and frightened at how lightly one world rests on the next.

When I think of my past now, it seems so far away, like India or the moon, farther almost than my future seemed to me then. And yet, when I turn my life, like a crystal, it shrinks in my hands. It fits in the space of a fist.

Be vigilant, my daughter; memory is the first story-teller. Anyone can simulate history, it's easy enough— there are classes of people, politicians and writers in particular, who have made it their calling. One can cata-log the years, write long lists that will recall small mo-ments. I can say Patent bedsheets "are eternal," or Napoli socks for men, or Polvo Tres Flores (I can still see it at the corner store, red boxes piled one on top of the other), and these things mean something to those of us who lived in a particular time at a particular place. I can sing that jingle, so overlaid with meaning, "Tasty until the last drop," and I am in the old city, passing an open window in an apartment where a man in a white T-shirt leans into a radio, adjusting the frequency, ahead of the terrible news. But these cues are open to corruption.

Now, late at night, when I can pick up the stations from Miami, I sometimes hear the same jingle and think the ghosts are speaking to me again.

I had long retained an odd memory from my childhood. It was neither traumatic nor happy. It was nothing, a pretty banality. But it would bubble forth unbid sometimes when I was quiet. And there I'd be: me yet a baby, turning to the lamp shade, where someone had pasted a little sticker of two purple feet. Those purple feet retained all their color in my memory throughout the years that followed. And often I found it disconcerting that I could remember that insignificant little sticker with such clarity of detail while the faces of so many I had loved have smudged and faded as if memory had worn them from the handling. I wondered about this aloud once to my mother. I told her I had hoped life would unfold like a book where each detail built on the one before it, all of it racing to a satisfying conclusion. But life is not a tidy narrative, she had said, pulling her hair back into a smooth bun. We learn this late. These scraps of memory that become untethered from the rest, flapping disconsolately in the wind, these memories are the most important of all. Memories like these remind us that life is also loose ends, small events that have no bearing on the story we come to write of ourselves.

*　*　*

Forgive me, my daughter. I have labored to construct a good history for you, to put down the details of your life smoothly; to connect events one to another. But my first efforts seemed false. And I am left with only these small shards of remembrances written on banners of wind.

After the triumph . . .

I don't know if I can describe to you the feeling of that time—it was the strange and dreadful excitement of a world turning, of everything staid and ordinary being swept away. The future rode a chariot and the people pressed together to watch it pass. We were all so happy then.

And those palms, eternal witness to the blowing winds. Oh Cuba my beautiful land!

How quiet was that first of January. An eerie quiet as if everyone were waiting to see what had really happened, no one quite ready to celebrate in case the dictator's abrupt departure had been a trick. But by the next day the crowds came spilling into the streets, as if a great convulsion had emptied every house in Havana. Men and women lined up past El Cotorro to the palace and out toward Columbia. Up and down our block, people hung the red and black July 26 flags. I didn't join any of the demonstrations. I have had since I was very young a terrible fear of crowds. But for days, from my little studio, I could hear the roar of the people, like a monster come out of the sea. Shouts, gunfire, glass breaking. There was hardly a block, it seemed, that didn't have at least one store that had been destroyed. Someone who wasn't there to see it, as I was, might say all that glass was broken out of bitterness or revenge or greed or even envy. All those explanations fail. Cataclysmic events, whatever their outcome, are as rare and transporting as a great love. Bombings, revolutions, earthquakes, hurricanes— anyone who has passed through one and lived, if they are honest, will tell you that even in the depths of their fear there was an exhilaration such as had been missing from their lives until then. In those first days of January, the air was clear, the nights were cool. It was like being young and knowing the joy of it as well as if one were old.

I remember passing a jewelry store on San Rafael in the early days of January. Every window had been broken. And yet all those jewels remained in their cases. I stood for a long time in front of the shattered glass, staring at a necklace adorned with a row of red rubies, like little drops of blood.

Toward the end of the month of January, my husband and I threw our party for the revolution. I thought at the time that the revolution didn't know what it wanted to be yet, but it was we who didn't know what we wanted to be.

Our house was made for parties. Even during the summer months you could put a small band out in the courtyard and the music would carry up to the top floors and at night the sound seemed to come from above and the stars seemed little points of light from the uppermost balconies.

I wore a dress of blue satin. I had spent the afternoon at the beauty shop, where the girls had gathered my long hair into a swirl at the nape of my neck and shaved the stray hairs and powdered me with lavender and rubbed my shoulders with rose oil. I had descended the stairs like a garden that night and I was happy for the murmur that rose, the faces that turned to me. I would relive the moment all that night; everything we do, all that we seek—beauty, wealth, even learning—is really at its heart a quest for power. Ever since I was very young, I was aware of the attraction I held for certain men, but it wasn't until I was older that I understood it. For a brief few years, I had the loveliness of youth and the knowledge of middle age and I felt I had found something unshakable and lasting. I was drunk on this power of mine. And that, too, passed and I came lastly to know how small this beauty had made my world, how little I really knew about living.

I danced with Calixto that night. Moonlight on the trumpets and the candlelight jumping in the cool January breeze. And then on toward midnight after the food and the drinks, we heard a distant siren wail and we waited until the sound was upon us. Car doors slamming. Shouting. Only Calixto was calm. Perhaps it had been a surprise of his, a visit that might delight his guests, raise his esteem in the eyes of his wife. . . . It seems like a dream now to retell this. I have not told this story ever. And now to put it into words seems unreal even to me. But it all happened; everything I put down here in the halting rhythm of memory, happened.

There he stands at the front door, his arm still in a cast. Walking through the door ahead of the others, his hair greasy, his uniform dirty, walking, eyes ablaze.

Comrade Guevara, my husband says in a too-pompous voice, I present to you Mrs. de la Landre. The revolutionary recoils slightly and our eyes meet very briefly. Much later, I will see this as the moment that we reach a private understanding with one another. But now, I don't acknowledge it, and instead am filled with a strange guilt whose source I can't quite place.

Ernesto took my hand and kissed it. I remember that Calixto laughed at this gesture, a little bird laugh. My wife, Calixto said, has a beautiful garden in the courtyard. You should see it. She raises ixoras and—her own particular specialty—miniature roses. He stopped and then added, On Thursdays, she arranges a dozen bouquets to take to the destitute sick in the children's ward. Ernesto bent at the waist at this last mention. And a beautiful heart, too, he said, still watching me.

That night, I lay next to my husband, whom I loved completely, who filled me and adored me, and I thought of this other man who frightened me and repulsed me with his smell and filth. I felt Calixto move next to me and then clear his throat. The revolutionary seemed very pleased to make your acquaintance, he said. I was quiet for a moment and then I said, He's vulgar, I know the type. And filthy on top of everything. The next thing Calixto said surprised me a little. He said, very slowly, the way he measured his words, Well, the way things are, it's not a bad idea to have important friends. I said to my husband that I hoped he wasn't in some kind of trouble. I'm not, he said. None at all. But I've agreed to do some work for them for when the trouble comes. Some writings, he said.

I closed my eyes then and listened for the sound of the wind, but the night had stilled and all I could hear was my husband's light breathing beside me, and long after it had deepened, I lay awake listening to the rise and fall of his breath.

Some days later I was in the courtyard, carefully trimming the small bush of miniature white roses I had managed to grow in a shady spot. It was a lovely tree and I was taken by the tiny petals of the roses that lay close and tight and would soon open, wide-armed, to reveal the soft darker center where the bud began. A friend of Calixto's had brought a small cutting of the plant years before from someplace in North America. I tended to it first in the cool of the home's interior and then gradually introduced it to the outdoors, moving the pot closer to the windows, then onto the porch and then out in the courtyard for an hour each morning in the winter, and then two, until by the time the cutting was big enough to be transplanted, it had been spending most of the day in the tropical sun.

I was talking to the plant as I pruned it, cooing softly to it, so that I hardly noticed when the front door rang. After a few moments, I heard Beatrice calling to me, and, a bit annoyed—annoyed also because Beatrice had developed this habit recently of yelling to me instead of walking to where I was—I wiped my hands on my pants and went to the door. A man introduced himself to me as Comrade X and said he had some papers to deliver from Comandante Guevara for Mr. de la Landre. I took the papers and thanked him. I asked him if he would like some coffee and he declined but he stood there not moving. You are Teresa de la Landre, then? he asked. Yes, I said, my hand on the door. The Comandante has heard many praises of your paintings. I smiled and nodded a sort of thanks, mute in my surprise. He has heard they are very beautiful, the man continued. I was stupid standing there. I think of it now and all the things I could have said.

When Calixto came home, I gave him the papers, and he walked to his study with them, closing the door behind him.

When the weather was good, I liked to walk the several miles to my studio, a walk that took me along the malecón and then up into the old city and past the grand department store, El Encanto, at the corner of Galiano and San Rafael. For many days after the revolution, while men filled the streets and stores took holidays, the windows at El Encanto remained unchanged, and as the days and then weeks passed I came more and more to see the rigid mannequins standing there as sculptures from another age.

I had been inside often and still remember the small pleasure of stepping off the tight streets of the old city and into the wide interior of the store. The inside, at least in memory, was very grand and clean, almost plastic in its perfection, and I imagined it a copy of the great department stores I had heard about in the United States. Jewelry, cameras. The most fashionable women in Havana bought their clothes there. As the revolution wore on, people began to whisper about the fate of El Encanto. Before long, they said the new government would issue a directive that the prices there would remain unchanged—almost as an unconscious nod to a capitalist past. And on hearing this I thought, with a smile, that every era builds museums to its secret longings.

*   *   *

El Encanto, like my studio, was a private comfort to me in those times. I dared not speak of the turn my heart had taken; I don't think I dared admit it to myself then. But I found that I was returning to the quiet spaces I had favored as a child: the closed doors, the shadows that can hide a secret afternoon. Alone with my paints, even when the panic seized me that I would never work again, I could retreat to the rhythm of the work, the smell of the oils, the light through the window.

I was working then on a large commission for a friend of Calixto's family. It wasn't the sort of work that I usually did, but it paid well. I was to create a total of seven panels that would depict scenes from Miami. The panels were supposed to hang in the lobby of a new hotel that was scheduled to open in a neighborhood that the man was developing in the Isle of Pines. I remember the day he came over with his plans. Moncada had already burned, the street fighting was flaring, a lot of people we knew were already moving their money to Miami, but this man was full of plans. He was going to call his neighborhood the New Miami, and it would rival anything in that American city, he told me. And I remember that in December—days before the revolution—he took out an advertisement in the magazines for his funny little development. The thing brimmed with hope: A new ferry! New airlines from Florida! And the spectacular Monkey Jungle!

It was after this that I took to calling him El Mono. He was a strange-looking man, with one of those faces that seems kind enough on first impression but that then reveal themselves to be hiding something else. His lips stretched over his mouth in a way that could be regarded as a smile or a barely suppressed baring of teeth. And his skin was so pale that, when he became agitated, thousands of tiny capillaries broke around his nose. I don't think I ever paid attention to any conversation he directed at me, so fascinated was I with the displays of his face. El Mono promised me a lot of money, twenty thousand pesos—this at a time when it cost eight cents to ride the bus—and I took the commission. But I had never been to Miami and so was forced to work from photographs and postcards, other people's interpretations. The strain of it would hurt me deeply. It was a hideous way to make art; but by the time I realized the magnitude of the lie, it was too late, the money had been spent and I had to work on. It's strange to think about it now. There I stood in my studio in Havana, day after day trying to paint Miami as if it were a city of dreams; more truly, it was a city of lies.

I spent a full week staring at these photographs that El Mono had brought me, trying to decide on seven scenes from all those images—the long flat beach, the buildings that sparkled at the end of the bay, the canopy over the white homes of Coconut Grove. I returned again and again to a photograph of a couple standing by a palm tree in front of an old hotel. It might have been a worn image except for the white, empty expanse of sand surrounding them and the way the woman held the man's arm, her fingers bent a little as if she were hanging on with fear. And the man's eyes had something— not a sadness exactly, but a kind of weariness that I couldn't understand and that therefore interested me. I placed the photograph on a stand and studied it day after day. The bent fingers, the downturned eyes, the lonely beach—one could paint this as a speck of black on a bright yellow background. And that old hotel, so straight and neat.

I thought the photograph, with the mystery of the man's eyes pulling at that happy scene from below, might prod me to make a true painting. But I could not seem to put down the first stroke. I went through the photos of Miami, thinking maybe to start with another scene. But the more I looked at the photographs the more they looked as if they were from an alien place, a place of the imagination. The revolution came and we were into January and then February and I still had not completed the first panel.

So it was that I was very absorbed in my work one early morning when the wind whistled down the alley, rattling windows as it went. If I heard the door open behind me, I made no note of it. There was a group of boys who lived on that floor who were always scurrying about, and I had taken to leaving the door unlocked rather than have to listen to their knocking. Perhaps I thought they had wandered in, as they sometimes did, to watch me paint. I heard footsteps. And then that smell, like wet leaves, old earth, metal.

I turned quickly to him, and maybe I gasped. He told me later I had gasped, though I have no memory of this. I remember only seeing him there and the strange feeling that it occasioned in me, because, except for the very brief moment at my house, I had not really taken a good look at him in person. As he stood before me he seemed very much the man in the photographs, and at the same time not at all him. Of course, there are the things that a photograph can't capture. The smell, yes. But also a roundness, a totality. A man whose full face seems gentle and kind may reveal himself something altogether different in profile. Gestures, movements—all these things go into an image of a person, or even of an object.

He was so alive, a man of breath and skin, and as I stood there with my paints I saw that within this life of his was contained also death. I would come to read his death

Ana Menéndez

in strange places: in the stories he chose to tell, in his walk, in the breath that caught in his chest as if a terrible parting were already wrenching at his heart. But even before all that, even before I knew him, that day in my studio, I could see the death that gently draped him.

I don't remember what I told him. Something trite that I later came to regret, no doubt. I have a recollection of him laughing. He pointed to a drawing in a corner and asked me what it was. It was a half-completed painting of an orchid, I told him, for a friend. He wore a strange smile, as if I were a child and he were about to scold me for a transgression. After a moment, he turned from me and walked to the canvas. I remember watching him walk that first time and thinking that some people move with such ease in this world that it is as if they had lived in it for many lifetimes before this one. He stood some moments before the unfinished canvas and then turned back to me and with that same smile said, Is it really necessary to make it so beautiful? I didn't smile back at him. I remember being uncomfortable with his familiarity. And also having the sense that he was mocking me. I responded with something absurd; I think I said, Yes, that's the way it is. And, suddenly sweating, I picked up my brushes again, which was a rude thing to do, of course. I began to dip the brushes into the paint as he stood there. Finally I looked up and said that it was a great honor, his visit, and asked if there was anything he needed. Imagine. What a thing to say to this man. But he was calm and didn't take advantage of my nervousness. He said only that he had heard of my paintings and wanted to see them for himself and that I should remember, in my work, that glory comes through struggle. I smiled a little bit. He walked around the studio for a while looking at various paintings, sometimes stepping back, sometimes picking one up and running his hands slowly down its length. I watched him move in my space and this time there was no color in the throat, no sound; only a sense that the days as I knew them were ending and that something new was waiting beyond the burnt edges.

That night I turned and turned in a hot bed. I had let this Argentine with his funny accent and mocking smile humiliate me. He smelled like a beast of the forest. Who did he take me for? When I closed my eyes, I fell instantly into a shallow sleep where no dreams came, only patterns of colors, sliding and laying themselves over one another. I grasped at the colors, sure that there was one that no human eyes had ever seen. Sometimes when I was about to fall asleep I had fantastic ideas such as these, visions that I could not later recall or put to paper, yet that when I awoke seemed to fill me with a new knowledge. I knew these visions still danced and fluttered at the dark edge of my imagination and lived and were fed in my waking life.

I awoke in the middle of the night. Calixto lay sleeping beside me. I remember that the windows were open, the night being cool, and that I thought the sound of the sea, liberated from the din of day, floated into the room. Everything was bathed in the blue light of night. The white curtains billowed in the breeze. To me, still half steeped in sleep and forgotten dreams, the house seemed suddenly enchanted. I left the bed carefully so as not to disturb Calixto. Downstairs I poured myself a glass of water, and it seemed to me that the water had never been so delicious. I walked through the darkened house until I came to the courtyard, where I stood for a long time. In the night light, my familiar flowers grew exotic and strange. I stood watching as they swayed back and forth, back and forth ever so gently, and a shiver spread from the center of my back down to my fingertips.

All that following week, I had to keep fighting the urge to fill the canvas with blue spirits and monstrous flowers, the world now small and only partly real. I listened for every sound in the hall, but that week even the children were quiet. On Friday, I left the studio early and went for a walk. The air was still cool, the sky blue, and it occurred to me that for us in the tropics, winter is the season of renewal.

Small pink flowers burst from the smallest patch of grass, the leaves of the flamboyan were a young, glossy green, and even the broken glass on the sidewalk, alive with sunlight, spoke of new things. I walked through the Chinese neighborhood, with its narrow crooked alleys, the hanging laundry, the water that sluiced through the streets. I had no purpose in my walk, was looking for no one. But the streets were full of the young bearded soldiers and I couldn't help the turnings of my heart when I saw one from behind.

After a time, I found myself in front of the old offices of *El Tiempo*. The sidewalk in front of it was still littered with paper and filing cabinets and desks. The windows had all been shattered and I supposed that vandals had taken whatever of value had been inside. There was an incongruous little ladder in front of the place, and I stood wondering what it was doing there when suddenly the entire scene went flat. It was a strange effect, perhaps brought on by my anxiety over the commission, and it lasted mere seconds. But for that small moment the scene was reduced to a surrealist impression—the ladder, the bits of newspaper, the wonderful sign above it all: TIEMPO. I wonder now if we had not all gone slightly crazy by then. And when I started to laugh, for no reason other than my own irrational one, the small group of men who had gathered in front of the ruins laughed with me.

I stood there at the destruction of *El Tiempo*'s offices for a very long time, drawn to the strange, disordered beauty of it and of the city. It was as if we had performed an ancient bloodletting on ourselves and afterward everything would be well.

I took the long way home, walking up Carlos III so that I could stand for a while in front of Castillo del Principe, but when I got there I found the place full of military and the view mostly ruined, so I continued past the hospital up and over one street and before long I came to the house with a square tower and a turret and ornamental scallop shells. Two Doric columns supported a thin balcony. I recognized it as Eddy's house because of the small crowd of die-hard Orthodoxos standing in front of it. One of them, a clean-shaven man in his thirties, carried a sign that said, THIS IS MY LAST CALL!

The next morning, I arrived at the studio very early. The light was slanting in and it was almost cold. I stood there in the spot of sunlight for a while. Always, when I stood before a canvas, I was seized with a terrible fear, and I would do anything—order my brushes by number, sweep the floor, fiddle with the blinds—to avoid going back to the work.

Entire days could go by with me not coming within two feet of a painting, and on those days I would hate myself so intensely that I could scarcely glance in a mirror. How worthless I felt much of the time! Sometimes I wondered if I painted more to stop these terrible feelings of irrelevance than I did out of any joy for the work. But that morning, after standing for a while in the slanting light, I went to the canvas hungry, eager, as never before, for the touch of the brush, the smell of paint, the heat of work. I painted all day, without even stopping for lunch. The next day was the same. And the next. Over the course of that week, the Miami Beach scene changed gradually, rather like a storm approaches, and almost without my willing it, the couple on the beach came to be framed by palms blown sidelong in the wind and white ocean sprays—bits of life that I took from my own experience, the same white spray that came over the malecón in bad weather. By the end of the week my arms and neck ached and I spent a long time in a warm bath thinking that there was no way that El Mono was going to take that panel and lying there in the water all the strange exhilaration of that week—for I had genuinely thought myself a genius—ebbed away and I was left with a profound and inexplicable sadness. This melancholy seemed to pull me closer to its breast minute by minute. The next morning I spent several hours unable to move, staring only at the sliver of light through the closed blinds, and in my imagination the light was a solid thing gently trying to pry open the windows.

Some days later, I returned to the studio. I walked as before, taking the route that took me past El Encanto. I stood in front of the display windows for a while as I had done so often, and this little familiar routine seemed to comfort and settle me—the mannequins so clean and perfect in their pillbox hats and smooth limbs.

But at the studio, I opened the door to the old dread. I walked around, opened the blinds. After a bit of this, I stood in front of the canvas that I had finished in such a frenzy of excitement. The lines now seemed crude, the colors garish. I began, very quickly, to paint over everything and ended, finally, by taking a planing knife to the entire canvas. I tore it to shreds with long wide movements and after lay exhausted on the small mattress in the corner of the room.

When I returned home, tired and exhilarated, I was surprised to find Calixto there. He was lying on the couch with a small glass of rum beside him. Without even saying hello, he said, You just missed your revolutionary admirer. I stopped where I stood and Calixto may have taken the change that came over me as ominous because he said, Listen, we have to try to engage him, them. Why did he come? I said and was relieved when my anxiety

came out as anger. Calixto held up a packet, Some work
for me. What work? I said. Calixto only shook his head.
To this day, I'm not very sure what it was they were asking him to do. I suspect it had nothing to do with the
packet of worthless paper that Ernesto or his secretary
dropped off now and then. I think they were keeping an
eye on him. No one quite understood his writings to
begin with. And already a thin black core of doubt had
begun to burrow into the revolution's heart.

I told Calixto that I never wanted to see anything again
of that man. He's a communist and a charlatan, I said, and I
just don't like him. And on top of that, I added—somewhat
to my horror—he's a womanizer; I can spot one from
three leagues. Calixto laughed at me. You're wrong there,
he said. He's forbidden his men from going to the dancing
halls. And, Calixto continued, when he learned that a few
of them had girlfriends they were seeing in the bushes
around La Cabaña, he ordered them to a mass marriage
ceremony. He's quite in love with his woman. The word is
that they'll get married soon. When I heard this, I walked
very slowly to the couch and sat next to Calixto. Everyone
knows about the girlfriend, Calixto continued, me barely
hearing. She's blonde and beautiful. I guess the Argentine
rebel is not so revolutionary in his taste for women. From
Batista to Guevara, Calixto said, they all like them blonde
and beautiful.

In March, the weather began to change. I had not heard from El Mono for some time, but every morning, I went to the studio to work on the panels. Why I returned again and again I don't know, for I found the work difficult and often recoiled from the canvas with such obvious disgust that many times I wondered if there were not better work for me someplace else.

Many mornings, I did nothing more than stand at the window watching the monstrous clouds of the coming summer cast shadows on the scene below, the soldiers like small insects under the immense sky. I spent entire days like this, rarely working, standing at the window, watching the wind turn the white sheets hung out to dry between buildings, and often when the wind caught them and billowed them my own heart would swell and I would think again of Ernesto.

In March, too, was when Beatrice left us. Only Calixto was surprised. She had taken to shouting at me from across the house. And at the same time, she had begun to slink around corners with great secrecy. I would step into a hallway and be startled by the sight of the woman standing in a shadow, watching me. When I asked her what she was doing, she would only say, Resting, madam. Later, she began to add, incredibly, This house is a lot of work, you know. After a while, it began to seem to me that she positioned herself around the house with the express purpose of startling me. Strange things happened when she was around; it was as if she disordered my thoughts. I remember one day I had been in the courtyard tending to my roses now that the heat was coming when I heard a car pull up to the house. I heard it quite distinctly, and with my heart in my throat I stood and wiped my hands and ran to the door before Beatrice could get it. But when I flung it open, I was surprised to find the street empty except for a small boy walking slowly up the side of the road with his books. Standing there, I had the sensation that the sky was bending down around me like an empty tunnel. I closed the door slowly, thinking, and when I turned around Beatrice was in a dark corner; she gave me such a fright that I mentioned it to Calixto that night. She left us three days later, after I had paid her for the month.

Years later, I opened the door one day to find Beatrice standing on the threshold. She told me a fantastic story about how she had had to leave because the security forces had asked her to spy on us. I never believed it. But she was thin and ragged, and I was at the beginning of a very bad state, so I welcomed her back.

She lives with me still, through many moves and seasons. Every other weekend, her daughter comes to visit. And then we stay up late, drinking beer out of little coffee cups and playing cards into the early morning. Sometimes the young woman will look up at me, a mocking smile breaking the line of her lips, and time shifts and I imagine it is you sitting before me and I allow myself a sorry old woman's wish to turn back the years.

One morning I wake early, before daybreak, with an aching so long suppressed that I think I will tear at my skin. In the dark, I find my way to the front door, glowing blue in the night. I step through it as through a wall of water. I float above the street, until I reach the far shore of El Morro. I sit on the ledge of my dream and gaze at the fortress that rises from the other shore like an old pale moon on the harbor's edge. I prefer the streets at night. The Havana day gives up too much. It is a lonely streetwalker telling all, showing all before the sale is done. Night in Cuba, like sleep, quiets detail, erases the inessential. It crouches about the edges, polishing the bones of the city like water lapping on a dock.

I stand across the harbor and look on La Cabaña. Its stone walls are lit with blinking torches, like eyes opening here and there in the impenetrable facade. How many untold stories behind those thick stone walls. How many muffled dreams. And yet, from the watery distance the ancient walls seem soft, like cork, like something I could caress. I know he is inside, can smell him from the far shore. He has just finished a trial, is sitting next to Duque on the bench. So many prisoners, hundreds, thousands, some without names, some who beg, eyes red before him; some who stand still and straight, already dead. I watch their hands, pale and trembling, watch them walk slowly toward him as if they were afraid of tripping. As if some unseen object lay before them, sent down from that other world that opens its doors tonight.

Outside the fort, bonfires cast alternate shadows on the white statue of Christ that looks over the water. Two figures crouch at the base, hiding between the veils of light and dark. They meet, come together. Even from where I stand, I can hear the soft play of grass beneath their bodies.

The entire world bends down to touch me—the stars and the invisible clouds and the limbs of trees all draw closer and closer. Soon dawn will come, dusting with pink the tops of the cathedral, polishing the capitol dome. And then it will move down to the alleys, like a drunk returning home, slowly tracing its steps, illuminating the city corner by corner before bursting out over the rooftops, flooding the ocean again with its reflection.

This photo I've given you—look at it. The camera has
caught him mid-sentence, his shirt half-buttoned, leaning
forward. He is both reduced and inflated on the page. A
grand enough person to have his photo taken. And yet his
face is flattened, frozen, his eyes dead in the camera.

First he was a distraction, a snaking shiver on the smooth surface of the day.

When the new *Bohemia* came, I sat on the couch, turning the pages quickly, until I came to his photo. I searched the papers, the foreign magazines. Each time I came across his image, I lay there looking at his face for a long time; then I carefully tore out the page. Over the next weeks, I did the same with other photos I found. I trimmed them and stacked them carefully in a box in my closet with these recollections. One night, when I again awoke before my husband, I went to the closet and pulled out a photo from *Bohemia*. I sat cross-legged on the floor of my closet, the only light coming from the half-moon outside as I traced the outline of his dark mouth.

I begin to study my own face in the mirror. I am still a young woman. But by the conventions of the time, I should have long ago left behind the flatteries of youth to settle into motherhood and home. The men still look from the corners, bend forward in their chairs. And yet, now and then, as I regard myself, I see the frontier of a shadow advancing and, in my eyes, the understanding that whatever else I might make of my life, whatever joys might broaden a day, time itself is irrevocable.

One day, as I stand in front of El Encanto as has become my custom, a wind unusual for that time of year suddenly picks up from the sea. I hear it first in the high rustling through the buildings and imagine the sea rising white over the sea wall again. First, it brings a pleasant coolness and the smell of salt. But then the wind gathers force until it cries its way around the corners of the city and blows bits of trash deep into the narrow alleys. From far away comes the sound of sirens and then the wind banging shutters and metal cans and I become slowly aware of daylight retreating behind a dull haze. I stand still at the corner, facing the avenue down to the sea, and my heart begins to pound. The streets around the store are deserted. Not one face in a window, nor a body on a balcony. It is as if the whole city has been warned of some catastrophe that only I now stand ignorant in the midst of. The trash blows about me, the dried leaves. I gather my things, holding my skirt down from the wind, and as I run through the empty streets I feel the first grains of sand rubbing against my face.

For two days I lie in bed with a high fever. Calixto comes to sit by my side, stroking my hands. He stays by my side and bathes me in the mornings until one day, I open my eyes and the sun is inside the room and I know I am cured. I sit in bed, all heaviness gone from my head, and watch a flock of white birds fly past the window. And beyond the birds the green leaf of the ceiba and beyond that the blue sky that cradles the clouds and arches over the world and whispers to me a sharp and infinite rebuke to my secret longing.

And then one day I pass a store and stop at a familiar voice, the Argentine habit of shuffling a word's accents so that sentences seem disconnected, even subversive. I stand for a long time by the radio, again with the sense that the radio voice is hollowing a tunnel in the day for me, everything bending close.

We can keep on making plans like that, he says into my ear. But when we come to drawing up a balance sheet—that is, to comparing all we want with what we can do—we see that this cannot be done.

Then there is a long silence before the commercials return.

That night I burn again beneath the sheets. Someone has gathered up time and compressed it to a whisper. Behind my closed eyelids I watch the squares of colors bend and fold over one another, each a new shade of red. It is good to say things clearly. And I struggle to identify the voice in my ear. I wake, covered in sweat. In the dark I find my way to the courtyard and stand staring over my garden. The house has taken on a softer feel since Beatrice has gone. Its lines have blurred. Calixto complains about dust on the cabinets. But I begin to welcome the fraying edges, everything slightly askance, all the baubles of the house having abandoned their usual place. It is a moonless night and very dark and for a moment it is as if someone has pulled a shade down before my eyes.

Two days later, I go to the university, where he is to give a speech. I watch from far away. Slowly, I make my way to the front, through the throng of bodies, the naked skin of young men and women warm and slick against me as I pass.

At the front. Does he see me?

The air of freedom is in fact the air of clandestinity, he says. But no matter: It adds an interesting touch of mystery.

The woman I once was is walking down Obispo.

I've gone to do my shopping. Look, I'm wearing the green dress, the one with the full skirt and the big white flowers. My dark hair turns in the wind. A man whistles, of course; I am used to this. It is why I wear the dress and let my hair hang loose, though I pretend not to see the faces that turn to me. But really, I don't know any other kind of life. Assume that all women feel this. The attention has already burrowed its way into my sense of the world. I've known fear and disappointment, but still I cannot imagine indifference.

It is early, most of the city still asleep. I like to walk the streets when they are quiet. Sometimes when the cobblestones glisten with dew and the first breezes stir in circles around the sun, I think that yes, there is a place for me, the way there is a place for the birds that alight every morning on the first banyan in the square. There is a place for Teresa de la Landre.

I begin to walk to my studio and then hesitate. In this moment, a man selling peanuts begins to cross the street; a boy carrying five loaves of bread reaches out to steady the uppermost one. And at the corner, a jeep idles. The window in the back lowers. He is inside, motioning to me.

A kiss. The first parting of flesh. Everything that comes later is sweet elaboration. The first kiss is more intimate than the naked bed; its small perimeter already contains the first submission and the final betrayal.

The more I write, the more I remember, as if the words moving across the page were a wind blowing away the dust of years.

There were many sleepless nights when I lay in bed absolving myself ahead of my sins, arranging my memories so they might assist in the deception. I remembered the night I had returned from visiting my cousins at their farm. Calixto had waited for me with a vase of roses and told me how lost he'd been. Later that night, while he slept, I walked down to the kitchen for a glass of water and noticed, just fleetingly, that someone had moved our wedding album from where it always stood atop a writing desk in the hall. The next morning I found it hidden on a low shelf and moved it back. A year later, when I had returned from another trip east, I noticed after a party, as I was arranging flowers on the desk, that the wedding album had been hidden again. I didn't think anything then. It is very difficult to perceive one's life as it is. It is only in retrospect that we come to understand what our mind knew all along, not from a mystical understanding of the universe, but from the slow accumulation of fact that the waking self doesn't have the heart to accept.

Or it could be that I was merely knitting the thread that led back into my justifications and forward into my falling. Calixto seemed to me in those times parched, re-moved, as if he had discovered a way to subsist on words alone. When I moved to kiss him, I felt a seizing up, as if he resented my hunger. But it could be that this is the way that I began to remove myself from him. I wonder now if people don't make up their reasons for deception after the fact. And that what truly leads us into the arms of another lies beyond our comprehension.

The buildings on the malecón face the sea with boarded windows. The grass is dead from the heat, the flowers are dead. The only color comes from the red paint on the whorehouse door, the pale, weathered blue of a window frame, the pink of morning beginning in Oriente. The heat seeps in everywhere like sickness, like an ordering force occupying hidden courtyards, decreeing sleep, slow movements. Heat inside the dried-out stems of a crocus, in the powdering space between the sidewalks, inside the green leaves already going pale from suffering.

I imagine it all first: My skin is hot glitter in the sun and I long to peel it off, layer by layer. Ernesto follows me home to where my husband is just now getting up to go to work. He watches Calixto kiss my silent body. I wake and turn, and he is waiting. I am raw, burned; I am in the time of life when to feel is the purest truth. No words, but the slip of his tongue like an island of madmen. Adrift, searching.

I begin, even at that moment, to remember everything. I embalm the memory while it yet breathes. I forget everything else, that Ernesto is newly married and that my Calixto is kind. Strange thoughts torment me. I feel the doorknob before it reaches my hand. I hear the sobs of a mother in Holguin. I smell the Antarctic sea, salt ice and sharp. I know everything before it happens. And still I turn to him. Let him press his body against mine.

Already I knew him from long ago, had stood many years with him watching the moon set and rise again. His lips full and moist where palm trees grew and the peasant women came to be filled. In the long night that followed, the stars spun and his voice sang from the mouth of a shallow stream.

Together, we climb the stairs to my studio. Everything is new to me again. I notice for the first time the smell of cooking, the sound of shouting behind closed doors, the crowds in the street. The stairs we climb curve and turn, curve and turn. We walk through several narrow passage-ways and into a hallway that turns again onto a single door. The room is small and dark; its three windows looking out over a central courtyard; it is my studio, but now it's as if I were seeing it for the first time. Pushed against the wall are paintings I don't recognize.

I sweat in my flowered dress. In that small room, his smell overtakes me again: mountains and dirt and un-washed skin and heat.

I think back to the night I saw him first, the party in my house when I wore the dress of blue satin. Not love or lust—a thirst for him that I might die. And how I tried to be good and polite. To sit with my legs crossed. To laugh and be bright, to swallow my desire like bile in the throat. Thinking always that I must hold the balance of my world steady in my hands. Must not stumble.

And now in the small room, I at last take hold of the shifting, embracing it, tenderly first and then clutching into my fall.

His chest is narrow and racked from his illness. He whispers in my ear. Sweet sweet savagery. Time dismantles in our hands. I sleep and wake to his mouth. And then the sharp breath of knowing. He has entered my life to stay, burrowed deep into my lungs so that every gasp will bring me back to today: the pale desert settling its eternity into the far grooves of the earth, without end or design.

Later, I wake beside him. He sleeps and I watch: His lashes spill over the white skin of his face and I think of beauty that time doesn't alter, of marble statues that are always cool to the touch, carvings that come to life at night. His mouth, his mouth, is parted over his straight teeth and the thin hairs from his rebel's beard curl over his lips. Those lips defiant even in sleep.

Outside, the shouts of men returning from their labors. The blinds are blue with light beyond the window. Gunfire sounds, or thunder, and then it is quiet again and I am still, listening to a lost bird insisting at the window. And yet he lies, lies still, his breath easy, almost silent, with none of the gasping I will come to know. His arms are bent beside him, fists clenched. I follow his bare chest to where his ribs sink low to the sides. Small bruises mottle the skin on his stomach like leaf shadows on the valley floor.

I lie close to him, lie still and quiet next to him. In sleep, he moves his arm to embrace me, in sleep he rises again from the dead. Perhaps he dreams of someone else who comes to him in the night. I rest my head on his shoulder, my face in the rise of his chest. I whisper that it doesn't matter. That nothing matters. I breathe the moist soft of his beard and listen to the blood pumping beneath the rise in his neck.

He opens his eyes and watches me, propped on one elbow.

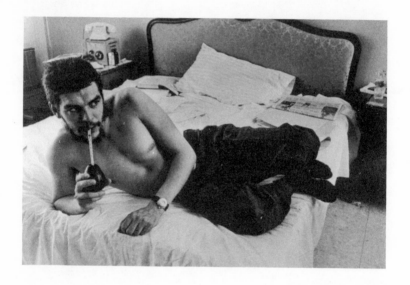

I move to kiss him, part his lips with my tongue. He murmurs, moves his hand down my spine, down. He pulls me onto his body. I let myself sink onto him. He looks up at me; My love, he murmurs. The light is beginning to fade from a window that now catches our reflection between its blinds. I am above him, watching him, this man who is not a hero or a photograph; who is only warm, smelling of moss ground, his body before me, freckled and soft, his skin tacky to the touch with dried sweat. He blinks slowly. He grabs my hair with one hand and pulls. Pulls down, gently, his other hand in the small of my back. He lets go and embraces me, brings me down to him so that I can feel his heart beating now against my chest. He turns me onto my side. He caresses my hair now, moving slowly, the motion of his hand a mirror to the motion of his body. Slowly I return to myself. I follow his movements. We watch one another. His breathing changes. He closes his eyes and draws me close, a great catch in his throat like day's dying into night. When he speaks again, it is with a voice that comes from worlds away.

The red in the sky is fading over the city, ebbing away behind the buildings. He says he will be back in two days. If I want to see him. Yes, I want to see him. He doesn't kiss me. He is back in his uniform, a different man now, sitting in the back of a jeep.

And this car, I say, where is it from?

We recovered it from La Cabaña.

Recovered?

Yes, he says, we took it back. You can say stolen if that is what you like. To conquer something we need to take it from someone else, he says. And it's good to say things clearly and not to hide behind concepts that might be misinterpreted.

The house is almost dark when I return. I change my clothes and wash quickly. I close the blinds, leaving the room dark, and settle into bed. A sudden joy takes me. I make an inventory of my body, discover only pleasant memory in the crook of my knees, in the muscles of my arms. And nothing that could be called guilt. Not even a sand's worth in the sloshings of my heart.

The door downstairs opens and then Calixto's voice is calling up to me. I lie very still. Teresa! His voice outside the door and then suddenly he is standing there in the light of the hallway, his face unrecognizable. I close my eyes into a thin crack and bring my hand to my head. Oh, Teresa. He comes to me and takes my hands. Oh, oh, you are so warm. Too warm. He touches his hand to my forehead. I am weak, I say. And maybe at that moment I begin to feel the first flutter of regret.

Calixto moves aside the covers. He holds his arms out to me and I sit up. He raises my nightgown over my head. I sit naked, eyes closed. I let my husband lift me. I feel myself rising from the bed, light, inconsequential. Calixto carries me to the bathroom and sits me on the tufted chair while he runs the water in the tub. I was surprised, he says, to find the house so dark. It frightened me. He speaks with his back to me, running his hand back and forth beneath the stream of water. I suddenly thought you had gone, that something terrible had happened. He stands and puts his hand to my forehead again. Then he lifts me, his arms beneath my naked legs, supporting my arching back. He lowers me slowly into the water.

He sits in his good gray pants at the edge of the tub and soaps a sponge and begins to bathe his wife. I close my eyes and sink lower into the water. The rough sponge over my forehead, down my face, beneath my neck. The sound of the water being wrung from the sponge. The sound of water displacing. The sponge across my chest, around each breast, down beneath the water. How do you feel? I open my eyes. Sweat has darkened Calixto's hairline a dark blond. His eyes are greener and brighter than I remember. He holds his hand out to me and leads me out of the tub. He wraps me in a towel and brings me back to bed. I whisper, I am new now. A happy weariness comes over my body inch by inch, an exhaustion so complete that it takes hold of me suddenly. Within seconds I am inside a deep black sleep.

Late in the night I wake to the soft flutter of birds' wings. At first I don't know where I am, imagine myself back in the shabby studio, and I draw my breath. Gradually I return to the bed where I lie, my own white room, the lace curtains over the windows that now let in the moonlight.

The next morning, I butter Calixto's bread slowly and hand it to him. I watch as he dips it into his coffee without even looking, his eyes on the newspaper before him. A toothpaste shortage now, he says and arches his brow. He doesn't say anything more and neither do I. Politics do not interest me.

Calixto puts his paper down and finishes the bread. He kisses me on the cheek. I knew we could cure you, he says and smiles. I sit at the table for a long time after. And then I pick up the breakfast things and take them into the kitchen and wash them one by one, glad for the hot water and the way it stings and reddens my hands back to life.

Once again I can discern the wind that brings rain, the smell of wet earth miles away. And this new awareness, I tell myself, is proof that what I am doing is right, for the world seems so new and lovely now and my place in it assured at last.

Every day I step into a new self. I walk the streets, where the trees whisper secrets and the flowers are so red and full that I wonder why the priests don't denounce them in their sermons. Some days, the clouds hang so low and heavy that I have to turn my face to the ground.

One afternoon, in the middle of a downpour, lightning falling with thunder on its heels, I step outside my studio and begin to walk in my green flowered dress, the water soaking first into the fabric and then running cool under my skin. The streets are empty, shutters closed on the houses. No one passes me. I have the sensation of being the last survivor of a cataclysm.

When I pass El Encanto, I almost weep at the sight of the plastic mannequins who have never known love.

I begin a new painting of the couple. In this one too, the woman is gripping the man's arm so that though she is smiling, her bent fingers suggest something else. But the man's eyes are still giving me trouble. I have painted them over and over. One time the eyes are too melancholy, another time too round with a happy memory.

The couple stands in the middle of the canvas—no beach, no palm tree, no hotel. Not even their bodies are completed. Someone coming upon the painting suddenly might imagine that the man and woman were slowly stepping out of the white nothingness. Though this is not how I see it. They are not coming out of the canvas, but out of me, as if my fingers were bleeding beneath the surface.

I have given them names: Mina and Sami. Though these are probably not American names. Probably I heard them on the radio. But to me they are Mina and Sami. Even though I am copying, I feel that I am inventing them. And I am; already Mina's face is a little rounder, a little echo of my own mother's; already I am turning her into a daughter of mine. And Sami is himself, but someone else, too, someone who is living inside me.

I still hear him next to me, weeping for the solitary individual who defends his oppressed self through art. You react to everything, my lovely Teresa, as a lone warrior; your only aspiration is to remain untarnished. What are you trying to free yourself from?

He is not wearing his uniform today. He is dressed in black pants and a white shirt, like the banker he is supposed to be. His eyes are tired. In the room, he opens a window. Across the way, a woman leans out of her window and looks into our room. Don't worry, Ernesto says, she's blind.

I laugh. He takes my dress off, still smiling. I unbutton his shirt. His hands on my skin, his breath, his smell. The bells of the cathedral. The singing of a lonely bird. And suddenly and without warning, I am overcome by an immense sadness. He sees this and stops. He sits me down gently.

He says that the love lives inside the leaving, the knowledge that everything ends. He says to me: When I lie next to you as you sleep, I look at your fluttering eyelids, the down of hair above your lip and I know that nothing lasts, that this very quality sharpens love. Nothing would make life sweeter than knowing the hour of its passing. He kisses me.

Then he lies back. I come to him and let my hair fall over his face as he watches.

After sleep, I rise alone. I find my clothes and dress slowly. I stand at the window. The sky has clouded over since morning and the light streaming into the courtyard now is muddy. The city is so quiet that for a bare moment I can hear the sea beyond the rooftops.

As a girl, I used to think the trains ran only at night. Then I came to understand that the wail of the train was like the light of stars: present in the day, but trumped, for the moment, by brighter objects.

When I turn, Ernesto is sitting at the edge of the couch, his legs spread out before him, watching me.

What are you afraid of?

I watch him. I have never considered this question. As a child I was afraid of the black nights, the duendes in the walls. But it was more than that. Because I continued to be afraid long after I stopped believing in duendes. I open my eyes and look at the man before me, his beard so close, the rough hair that moments ago had touched against my rawness. I am afraid of his going, of the black space he will leave when he vanishes from my life.

Of death, I say.

A shadow passes over Ernesto's eyes. A disappoint-ment. And then he smiles. Well, yes. I never thought of this answer. But death to me is more a regret, not a fear. Fear is one of the things that make us value life. But how can you fear the inevitable? It would be like fearing the dawn.

I nod. After a while, I say, Then I suppose I fear the dawn.

He kisses me and when I open my eyes, I smile, to let him know that I was making a small joke.

The next time I see him is one of the darkest days of the year, a closed, suffocating grayness. Ernesto is so tired. Days ago, I lay with him and thought that truth was something one might experience, like a catch in the throat. Now, the shadows; the hidden corners; his heart beyond reach. It is not his wife I imagine when I imagine his leaving. His loving dream holds neither one of us; his first desire is to wear furrows into the earth, uncover mountains and forests until he finds beautiful death waiting faithfully for him.

Ana Menéndez

We go down into the street together. I follow him through the narrow alleys. From above, the sound of pots and metal spoons, children crying. The sky is trying to brighten at the edges. Maybe we'll escape the rain, I say. We turn into a little street and cross into the next alley. I follow him as he turns left and we walk a while and turn right again. Another turn and already I am lost.

The heat and the afternoon have left me weak. I stop and lean against the unpainted wall of a building to feel its roughness against my skin. He begins to walk ahead and then turns back to me. He faces me and then presses his body to me, playful first, until something changes in his eyes. He whispers, and his breath is hot in my ear. His hands on my shoulders, pressing me back.

And then, without warning, the growling of dogs, coming fast on us. I press against the wall hard. He covers me with his body. Three ugly yellow dogs, fur matted, gray skin showing through patches in their coats. They snarl and snap at us, showing white shiny teeth. My heart is beating fast against his back. Ernesto lunges at the dogs, and they take a small step back and then come at us again. Go, go, he says. Up and down the alley, windows open. A woman leans out. Ernesto bends his face down. He kicks at the ground, lunges again at the dogs. This goes on for a long time. I am sweating and don't know if I'm shouting or just thinking of shouting. I'm breathing the dust Ernesto has kicked up. I'm pinned against the wall. And then he takes a rock and throws it, hitting one of the dogs in the leg. And another rock to the snout.

I hurt them, he says after. I was only trying to protect you.

When I was a boy in Cordoba, he says many days later, we lived near a sad neighborhood of cardboard houses. Here, among the desperate immigrants from the countryside, lived a legless man, the Man of the Dogs. He got about on a cart pulled by a pack of dogs as wild and suffering as he was. Every morning the crying of dogs would announce his waking as he beat them and cursed them to move faster.

The Man of the Dogs was the town attraction, he explains, much like El Caballero de Paris. Every morning, the cripple on his cart, spitting and raging and beating the dogs with all the anger he had for life. Every morning, the dogs crying and straining beneath the whips. One morning, the other boys began to run after the man. They threw rocks at him, and bottles, shouting, Rise up, Lazarus, rise up and walk! I pleaded with the children, who instead turned their taunts on me. I ran between the children and the Man of the Dogs. Stop! I shouted at the other children. Have compassion!

And you know what happened? Ernesto says. The man looked up from his cart, and his dead eyes were full of loathing for me. . . .

* * *

Listen, I say, a bird singing in mid-afternoon. He turns his face. His breath is slow. I tell him about summers on the farm in Cárdenas. About how the birds blackened the sky to nest. And how I used to climb the mango tree to lick warm sweet meringue from a bowl as the land beyond filled with shadows.

One afternoon in the summer, when it is so hot that we have to lie far apart on the mattress, not touching, Ernesto asks me why I never talk about my husband.

Out of respect for both of you, I say. And then, because he is waiting for me to continue, I say, You never talk about your wife.

What do you want to know?

Exactly what you've told me—nothing at all.

Ernesto is quiet. I lie in the dark and think that I think of nothing but after a while I understand that the image that has been forming inside the blankness is of her. I've never met her, though I've seen her photograph and heard it said that she is very beautiful. I try to think of other things, but my mind wants to linger here with her. I close my eyes and become her. Waking up to her husband arriving late again. She hesitates one minute, imagines she sees something in his walk. But then he is sweeping her up in his arms again, telling her beautiful things, telling her that she is beautiful.

Does he kiss her the same way? Does she wonder, like me, when she sits listening to the water run in the bathroom how a heart can divide itself so evenly?

After a long silence, I say, I know that you love her very much.

It doesn't bother you?

On the contrary. I love that you love, and I think better of you for it. We have it all wrong about love.

How do we have it wrong? he says.

That it has to be only one way.

He is quiet. When I turn to him, he has drawn his lips together.

Yes, nowhere is it written that a man and a woman must have only each other, he says. And yet . . .

He leans up on his elbow. And yet, he says, this is a dangerous way of thinking. He pulls me to him. If one might love whenever and wherever, it might follow that orthodoxy is an illusion. What's to prevent anyone, then, from cuckolding the state with any pretty idea that, on passing as he sits at a cafe, sets his mind aflame?

No, he says, and his hands are already over my skin. No matter how much we try, we will always love some things more than others. And some things we will love so much that we will honor them until death.

Years later, I was alone in the studio when I heard foot-steps outside the door. I stopped and stood quietly by the window. The knock on the door was rough and hurried, and I died a little to remember the times when he had entered so softly, blurring the edges of his arrival.

A man I didn't recognize spoke my secret name, the one that only he knew. He handed me a letter. After he left, I held the envelope in my hand for long moments. I wanted to wait. But I couldn't, and slowly I tore the seal:

> *Adored one, I am off to my fighting.*
> *I shall scratch the earth to make you a cave*
> *and there your Captain*
> *will wait for you with flowers in the bed.*

I carried the letter with me for months, opening it now and then to feel the ache in my chest again. Ernesto who had covered me with his hands, his touch like wading into a small pool only to find it deep and cool and sweet beneath the reflection.

Because your kisses live in my heart
like red banners.

I never stopped loving my husband. Because I never spoke of him to Ernesto—because I rarely speak of him to you—means little. We are always trying to see beyond the blurred outline of our fist; so we struggle to know the meaning behind what is said and not said. Like palm readers, we think truth is as easy as the lines that betray us. Calixto was a good man. There is no reason I should have gone to another. So I did. This is the only logic worth knowing. Another woman would explain that Calixto began to travel—that he was gone for months to Moscow, Budapest. That he was in Madrid the night you were born. The most vulgar notion of cause and effect that has nothing to do with the way the heart grows in advance of a meeting it has not imagined. I understand now that years before I knew him, Ernesto had already become my waking and my sleeping, my every thought; and there wasn't a moment that he wasn't with me, from the nights long ago when I sat listening to the old mulato at the piano, to this moment when I sit at a worn desk to write a blind letter to my daughter. Someday, maybe very near, you may wake one morning and not know whether you have opened your eyes or just begun to dream. Maybe you will ask, as I do, if one can really separate this world from the one written on angels' wings.

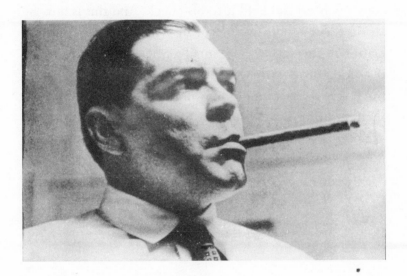

The last time I saw Ernesto, he was dressed as someone else. He was standing by the old banyan in the square, standing very straight. He was looking away, head slightly raised. A haughty businessman, a relic from the last age. All about him people came and went, no one seeing him. But I recognized him by the turn of his full lower lip, the way his forehead sloped over his eyes. You cannot fool a lover; a lover has mapped every contour, learned every hidden passage. A man cannot hide himself from a lover any more than he can hide from his own face.

He turned to me, and I walked slowly to him. The familiar smell beneath the white shirt, the same skin. He took my hand and held it to his cheek. And this is how he stood saying good-bye again, his voice small within the clatter of the square, too small a voice for the man he'd become. His breath was broken and hot. When he told me it was the last time, I only nodded. Adios, I said, commending him instead to the earth, the wide grass, the arching sky that we could still share. There is nothing final in love's good-bye.

But death. A Dios. Silence. That is a different forever.

For all his lusting after a beautiful death, for all his talk of not knowing what land would claim his bones, he clung, in the last moments, to the sweet air of the valley. Fear is one of the few experiences that make you value life, he had said to me. A fine phrase in the swelling chorus of youth. But what of the last hour? Coming out of the ditch, he hesitated. His hair was matted. He was hungry. Without his medicine, his breath came to him in hot spurts, his body surrendering ahead of him. But he hesitated. The beauty of this life yet held him—the bird that passed overhead, the sky and its clouds, the slope of the valley and the trees that clung to the side of the hills and, yes, even the animals that tore at one another beneath the boughs, the violent bleedings: the sorrows and joys. All that night, the radio going, the same news repeated over and over, not even the solace of a bulletin, the announcers grown bored by early morning. And still I sat and still I sat. And the next afternoon and the next, the news was the same.

Oh my Captain, my sweet Ernesto. And where the bed of flowers? Where the red banners? Gone away into silence, never to taste excellent morning again. Gone away to memory's tomb. Down, down, down into the dumb corridor of the saints.

Oh, but in the beginning how wide the sky had seemed, how infinite the horizon where we thought to rest our eyes for a season.

In the beginning . . .

Good Friday. The Passion winding through the Chinese neighborhood, the people lining the streets to watch, the pious women throwing themselves on the procession; Christ king, Christ savior. The crowd moving below the window as one. The cathedral bells sounding the noon death.

I was in my studio, my hands covered in blues and greens. The painting of Miami Beach rested against a wall, the man still sightless, the woman's fingers still pressing the flesh of his arm. I have read what you write about art, I said as I tried to fill the canvas, and I can see that you're not an artist. Instead of being insulted, he laughed. I'm not an economist, either.

I smiled. Art is not the things you say, I continued, now serious. It's not in service of this or that. Art is the unutterable, the self made of clay. I talked in this way for a while, with a gravity I no longer have, and he stood listening, silent, watching me. Art does not answer or listen, I said. It doesn't care for you; it doesn't want to comfort you, is responsible to no one; its being is all desire, all covetousness.

Ernesto came to me. Would you paint, then, he asked, without the promise that someone would see what you painted?

I thought about this for a moment. Yes, I said finally. I would paint for the painting itself.

He watched me and then laughed. No you wouldn't, he said. No more than anyone labors for the darkness. Your painting doesn't exist until someone sees it. Like the taste of the orange that resides not in the orange or on the tongue but in the coming together of the two.

With a rag, he wiped the paint from my hands, slowly, thoroughly. When he was done, he brought my hand, warm and red from the friction of the cloth, to his lips. He kissed my hand, and then pulled me to his chest.

Even after all these years, I remember everything with a supernatural precision, with a certainty that is not given to actual life.

He rubs my hands until they are clean and red and then he draws me to him and hugs me in long silence. We come apart and he kisses me, opening up new landscapes with his tongue. Eyes closed, I travel through a green tunnel, tumbling out into open country. The blinds are drawn, the air is hot and moist. He kisses me again and lets his hand slide down my back.

He whispers to me, Sometimes a love seems both familiar and utterly new. He undresses me slowly and sits me down on a chair. He kneels and puts his mouth to me, letting his tongue roam, softly at first, until I too can taste a new country. When he finally enters me, I think of nothing, not the stars or the budding flowers or the sun that beats down upon the earth as we make love.

Never before and not since have my thoughts marched so closely in step with the sensations of my body; I saw that the past and the future were written in smoke. And afterward, felt only the immense sadness of the world settling down into its old contours again.

We lay together and slept away the afternoon. I awoke to
his breathing. My back was to him and he held me very
close in his sleep. After a while I knew by the change in
his breath that he had woken also. We didn't speak. No
other sensation but his hands on my body, over my shoulders, my neck, over my breasts, around my hips. He felt
down into my warmth and then placed himself inside of
me and I arched my back to him, closing my eyes to the
touch that tore thousands of tiny fissures within me. I understood then how someone might ruin her whole life
for love, throw away family and ambitions, put her very
soul at risk, for this glimpse of the eternal that life has
tricked us with.

He wakes with a tremor from a little sleep.

I just spoke to an angel, he says. A magnificent angel drawn up in gold garments. Her hair flowed over her shoulders and still I recognized her by this curve here. He runs his finger over my hipbone. The angel said that I must kiss every mole on your body and then I would be forgiven.

He begins at my ear. I am laughing, sleepy. That tickles. Him kissing, moving, like water over my skin. The opening up that is like a surrender. And then the force that takes my breath. Everything falling away, the sky peeling back from the sun.

You are forgiven, I say.

Even for the sins to come?

Even those.

Later, he lies with his eyes closed.

In Peru, he says, the mountains are very cold, even in summer. But the Indians walk everywhere without shoes, their callused feet white and thick as boots. From a distance they look like great herds of llamas, moving quietly, slowly over the ridges.

When the Indians reach the top of a mountain, they deposit all their sorrows in a stone and turn that stone over to Mother Earth. The sorrows accumulate until they form a great pyramid. The Spaniards tried to do away with this superstition, but despite their best efforts the sorrows went on accumulating.

So? I whisper.

So, he says, the monks adapted themselves to the inevitable. With time, all across the mountaintops of Peru, little pyramids of stones rose into the thin air, each pile of sorrows marked by a small Christian cross.

I sit on a bench in the plaza. The peanut seller watches
me. I wait. After a long hour, he walks toward me, and I
look away. Some peanuts, madam? Something familiar in
the voice. I turn to him, take a coin from my purse. The
peanut seller tips his hat and hands me a white paper cone
of peanuts. Thank you. At your service, he says, but he
does not leave. Yes? The man you wait for, he says, he was
here this morning. I stand, angry. You have me mistaken
for someone else, sir, I am not waiting for a man.

As you wish, madam.

The next day Ernesto doesn't come to the studio. Or the
next. Only the peanut seller watching me as I cross the
street to my building. I begin to take a different route. I
remember his words, The love lives inside the leaving. I
paint and repaint, setting down layers and layers of color
that in the end only I will know about. When the painting
is done, people will look at it and sense a secret.

Weeks go by, or years. One morning, I am working
when the three sharp raps come to the door. Military
police—open at once! The voice is harsh, and for a moment I catch my breath. When I throw the door open, it

is Ernesto standing there, laughing. My heart still beating fast from fear, and now longing and relief. I had missed you so. Military police, he whispers. I close the door. Did I scare you, he says? And he kisses my lips and my cheek and grazes his teeth into the soft space between my neck and my ear. Tell me how I scared you.

A storm is thrashing about in the city. I shut the window and after a moment close the curtains. I find my way back to the mattress by touch. His breath the only sound. I move close to him, find his shirt and unbutton it. I follow the length of his leg to his feet and remove his shoes, his socks.

Yes, you scared me, I say.

Good.

I undo his belt, unbutton his pants, pull them down, together with his briefs. I run my hands back up through the hair on his legs, stop where they come together, lean in to take in the smell of him, the smell that is mine now, that means something else entirely, that is full of our secrets together. And I take him in my mouth, the pulse of his desire like words against my tongue. Speak to me this way. I listen for his breath and wait, caressing, waiting, thinking nothing, wanting nothing.

After, I lie beside him in the afternoon dark, listening to the storm, the heavy drops running down the gutters, splashing the courtyard below outside the closed window. The sound of water closes my lids. I sleep. When I wake, he is by the window. He has parted the curtain enough so that a pale light falls about his head.

He comes to me. I knew when I saw you, he says. I knew about these breasts, these hips. I knew you already. So I wasn't afraid of never having you because I had already tasted your skin.

I close my eyes when he enters me, always I close my eyes, though I try not to. I close my eyes so I may see only this. His coming to me each time for the first time, a door opening into a new country, the sound of footsteps—approaching or departing? I must concentrate. And now, the world tilting away; I am afraid I will cry out for him, tell him everything: how I desire him, how I would like to run away from him and how I must possess him forever. The rain falls in long sheets, and it is like the ringing of bells in the cathedral. When at last I open my eyes, he is looking away, his own eyes rimmed in red, exhaustion in the hollows of his face, like skull shadows coming up through the skin.

Loving Che was like palest sea foam, like wind through the stars.

Savior, murderer, brutal love of my own creation. In the dark, his necklace of bones in my mouth. Entire afternoons passing in the time it took to close a fist or open the slits of our eyes.

I am at the window, looking down over the courtyard. Across the way, a woman sits ironing white shirts at her kitchen table. One by one she takes the shirts out of the starch and lays them out in front of her. Her hand smoothing the fabric is almost a caress. She is speaking something to herself or maybe singing. I lean closer, but her lips are soundless. She moves the iron slowly, now and then stopping to poke the coals with a small stick.

When I turn back to my work, I find Ernesto standing against the wall. He has entered so quietly and now he stands watching me, arms folded across his chest like wings. Take off the necklace, he says, not harshly but without smiling. I hesitate. Why? Because I ask you to. I stand for a moment. Is the door locked? He nods. I take the necklace off. And the blouse, he says. I lift my chin to him. It has never been like this. Always he has taken off my clothes himself, slowly, teasingly, so that I have barely been aware of my own nakedness. Please.

I do as I'm told. I unbutton the blouse. I look back at him but he doesn't speak. I slip the blouse off my shoulders. The skirt, he says. It's a pin-striped skirt I bought a long time ago at El Encanto. I unzip it. And the slip, he says. I let it drop with the skirt. I'm in my underclothes.

It is hot, but the sweat on my skin makes me shiver. He has not moved. He is watching. He nods. I shake my head no. He points to me. Do it.

I reach back to undo my brassiere, the lace one that I wear in the daytime for him. And then, not wanting to show embarrassment, I bend to lower my panties. I roll them down as I go, and the movement of this last layer over my skin introduces me to a new anticipation. I stand bare-breasted and open to this foreigner, like some fetish of a woman, some stone carving from the mountains of his travels.

But he does nothing, only looks. For a long time, he looks. And then he walks slowly to me. Without touching me, he bends and picks up my brassiere, helps me with it. He lifts my leg, one and then the other, and pulls my panties up. He pats my skin, lingers at my waist. And then the blouse—hole by hole, he buttons it. He slides on my slip. He holds my skirt open so I can step into it, my hand at his shoulder for balance.

For hours after he leaves, scarcely aware of my hands, I work, charcoal staining my fingers like smoke.

I trace his face, lightly at first, the way memory returns, indistinct, held together by the barest outlines. And then I dig deeper into the paper, darken shadows, rub light into the places where his forehead protrudes. When I was younger, truth was a flat plane, dimensionless, weightless; and the white paper was more honest than all the false green pastures of paint, a single blade of grass more real for its ignorance of space, its vegetable disregard for eternity.

But now I know that this is also true: that I can conjure his features from dust, blacken the paper with fire-ash, and have him speak to me again, if only in this language of deaf-mutes. I can form his soundless lips to my memory and only I will understand why I have given him half a face, dissipated half his features over the wide world. This much remains of my own possession: this curl in the hair, this eye that turns down in sleep and sadness, this eye that narrows in private joy.

I sit back, a little tired, but also filled with longing, my heart beating fast, in the old way. I am still for a while, only the movement of my chest rising and falling. And then I take the stick of charcoal to my hand, pressing into the flesh of my palm. When I've darkened my hand, I move around my wrists and up the inside of my arm, casting myself in pale shadow. It's like the old days when I could trace a pen to paper for hours. I move the charcoal into my armpits, and my skin shivers beneath its tracks. I close my eyes, nothing but the soft dusting of coal, wandering gray. The hand of God painting my skin, tracing riverbeds in some ancient map. And now I am far away from myself, and the only thing connecting me to my body is this dusty string, this story forming beneath my fingertips.

Daughter of my heart: You must remember that all our walking is a stepping into the other. We enter rooms and canvases, we look into one another's eyes, we open packages, we travel into other lands. We laugh and taste with wide-open mouths and our hands seek to touch and hold.

So it was with Ernesto and me when we opened the door to the small room at the top of the stairs so we might enter different lives. My going again and again to him, wanting to be lost in his body, thinking that this next time it would finally happen. To feel him in my hands as one might touch one's own self in a lost afternoon. To explore, to conquer. To take hold of a lover, to live inside another's silence.

Oh my child, these secrets locked tight so long. Soon I will lie at the end of a long hallway where you will no longer be able to reach me. And I think now that you might be a child again and suckle my breasts, hold them in your tiny hands. That you might fold time and reenter me, light the dark corners of your memory, back to the place where you began.

Trimming my roses one morning, I recoil at the sound of the stem breaking. I sit with my head in my hands. A bullfrog calls to me across the grass and in the old ceiba a bird wakes. The tiptoeing of a beetle echoes with a giant's step. Beneath my feet, the ants churn up the ground and the sound of earth tumbling on earth blots out every other sound in the world.

At the studio, the portrait of the man and the woman sits where it has for many months. I know that I will never finish it. And for a brief moment, as if illuminated by a flash, I see the future waiting for me. I know that I will give birth to a girl and that I will send her away. I know that I will wait in vain for my lover to return, will wait even after he is dead. That my whole life will be this waiting, pure and hopeful, and the days and years will stretch no longer than the moment it takes a cloud to cross the night.

I'm in my studio the day El Encanto burns. I hear the explosion and run down into the street. Already the crowds are gathering, running past me, bumping me. The sound of fire engines. Screaming. I walk quickly. On Galiano, I stop. Ahead of me, El Encanto is burning, ugly, smoke-ash, smell of plastic. And the sound of glass breaking and breaking, up and down the front of the building, pop, pop, pop as the fire engulfs everything: the dresses from Paris, the gold jewelry, the transistor radios, the glass display cases, the white columns, the front windows. The front windows, with their pale mannequins. I come close enough so that I can feel the heat on my face. The flames take the mannequins, crawling up their stiff limbs like a caress, setting their hair aflame, and they stand, unfeeling, in the same old pose until they start to melt, the smile still on their painted lips. . . . The building is destroyed, and the only casualty is a worker named Faith, who had gone back inside to retrieve some paperwork.

I'm not going to lie to you, sweet Teresa, he says. My voca-
tion is to roam the highways and waterways of the world
forever, always curious, investigating everything, sniffing
into nooks and crannies, but always detached, not putting
down roots anywhere, not staying long enough to discover
what lies beneath.

Summer again, but the sky blue, Havana without rain for weeks. The heat pushing against the glass, no hope of release anywhere.

I prop myself up on my elbow. His eyes are closed. I run my hand over his forehead, pushing the hair off his face, run my hand over his brow and down along the corner of his eyes and the side of his cheeks and still he doesn't open his eyes. I run my finger across his mouth and bite back the desire to touch my lips to his. Down his mouth and through his beard, down to his throat, resting my hand there to feel the trembling of his breath.

He doesn't move. When we were still in the Sierra, he says without opening his eyes, we had a soldier named Eutimio Guerra. It shows you the little value in names. Because of war this man had not even a middle name. He was a coward and a traitor. When we found him out there was only one course of action.

Ernesto opens his eyes. Eutimio was down on his knees. He asked quietly to be shot. He retained some dignity, out in the open, under the sun, on his knees. There was no pleading or crying or any of the shows that make what needs to be done any more displeasing.

Ernesto pauses and turns to me. No one knows this, he says. It began to rain, the darkest deluge, all the sky gone black—the trees, the grass, our hands. The situation was . . . uncomfortable. No one wanted to do it. Eutimio had been a brother to us. There was nothing I could do. I had to end the problem myself, do you understand, Teresa? Myself, because no one else would do it. Quick as a breath. I shot him once, before he could blink, the .32 into the right side of his brain.

Ernesto is quiet. The rain falls in the courtyard. He leans toward me and whispers. Exit orifice in the right temporal. Orifice in the temporal, Che, the old doctor, whispers.

He gasped and then was dead. Do you think I liked that? Do you think I liked it? and he says this softly, all the anger gone out of him. So softly that it is like a question to himself.

When Eutimio was dead, Ernesto says after a long while, I began to take his belongings. His watch had been tied by a chain to his belt. I couldn't take it off, and I struggled with it. This was many hours after his death. And yet, Eutimio Guerra grabbed my hand. Yank it off, boy, said the dead man to me, what does it matter. . . .

But this is what I've never understood, Ernesto says. He was already dead.

* * *

We lie together, distant thunder closing in on the city. Neither of us speaks now. I rest my head against his back and listen to his breathing. Each breath coming soft and easy. We lie for a long time, me listening. And then a soft whistling on the exhale, like a distant warning bell. His exhalation begins to catch on itself. The muscles on his back tighten and then release. He lies still, and I know he is trying to control the breath. But the whistling grows, each new breath a greater effort until suddenly he sits up and leans forward. He takes my hand and then pushes me away. The muscles below his ribs pull in, the muscles of his face, his stomach. I stand and kneel in front of him. Your medicine, your medicine. He is still. His skin is cold. You are growing blue, I say; your medicine. My heart is beating fast. Your medicine, Ernesto!

I run to his jacket and go through the pockets until I find the syringe. I fill it the way I've watched him. His face so pale. A fallen little bird, thin panicked ribs pressing against his skin. My hands tremble. I hold the needle to his arm, but I can't do it. He looks at me, nothing in his dark eyes that could be called fear, only a confused resignation. I hesitate. His face so pale. And then I plunge the syringe into his skin, looking away as I empty the adrenaline into his blood. His chest quiets its frantic pulling. The whistling through his throat increases and then subsides. He lies back on the mattress. I sit on the floor and let my breath out slowly. Color returns to his face. He closes his eyes. When he can speak again, he says, My lovely Teresa.

I walk home alone. The afternoon is hot beneath the black clouds. A boy races by on his bicycle and the wind in his wake rustles bits of paper in the street. I walk, trying to calm my heart. Ahead walks a man familiar by the slope of his shoulders. His head is turned down to the ground as he walks, his hands in his pockets. When he turns down to the malecón, I speed up. I cross the street at a run, cars sounding their horns. The man lifts his head to look across the traffic at me and I see that it is no one I know.

Don't you understand, Calixto said to me before he left for Madrid, that the very word revolution is doomed to failure? Round and round and round, forever trapped inside its own semantic fortress, forced to retrace its steps for all eternity.

You were born in the middle of the night and your screams filled me first with awe and then with fear, this new stranger who'd come from me, this new person with her own beating heart.

Someday I would give you a good life. Someday when my lover returned. Someday I would become your mother. I was waiting. I sent you away from this island so that you might be free of its sounds and sweet airs.

I was waiting. How could I have been of help to you? Already, I read him in every move of your hands, smelled him on your sweet baby's breath. When you cried at night, I lay remembering the lost afternoons, how time had wrapped its eternity around us.

The night before my father's flight, I woke before dawn. The house was silent. Not even the sound of the wind through the eaves. I walked to your little mattress and watched you sleep. You were still, facing heaven, your arms outstretched. Your mouth was parted and your chest rose slowly. I kneeled next to you for a long while. I caressed your hair and I bent and kissed your forehead. I kissed your chin, brushing my lashes against your lips.

I kissed you and you opened your eyes, your face a breath from mine. You lay still, quiet, your black eyes looking back at me.

I was waiting, you see.

And then one day you appeared. Beneath my window, singing for me the poem that so many years ago your father had sung for me.

You appeared like a vision. And I could not move from where I stood. The years and the sorrows held me fast.

You and I are past forgiveness or understanding. I took a history from you and you returned carrying his memory in your dark eyes. I have suffered punishments enough. To you I leave these small words, these images stilled with a spirit that belongs to you. I leave you our failures together and also the private triumph of your own life, the beating in your chest of a love that endures.

Farewell.

Ana Menéndez

Farewell but you will be with me.

LETTER ON THE ROAD

I sat with Teresa's letters for a long time. I was not so removed from exile chatter that I didn't understand the implications of her story. Miami was not a city for romantic heroes; here, an association with the revolution was something to be hidden, denied, and ultimately forgotten. Any hopeful joy I might have felt at Teresa's words was tempered by the story that contained them. In the confusion I felt at that moment, I was moved to throw the entire contents of the package away and I may have actually stood with that intention. Instead, after a moment, I carefully restacked Teresa's letters and photographs. Barely aware of what I was doing, I packed them back in their box. I sealed the edges of the package with masking tape and then I found a length of twine and wrapped it tight. I pushed the box into a closet, setting it on the highest shelf.

Some days later, I drove to my old neighborhood. I had not returned since my grandfather's death and was surprised at how little the streets had changed, how familiar the houses seemed. There was the same porch and steps leading up to the front door and the window that I used to look out from, imagining the world that lay beyond, the people I would meet, the woman I would become. It was late afternoon, but the street was deserted. I parked across from the house. The driveway was empty and the blinds had been pulled down shut. Someone had planted red geraniums under the windowsills and the lawn was trim and green. I waited there, looking at the house for a long time, waiting for someone to enter or leave. I dozed for a while in the heat. When I awoke it was getting on toward evening. I sat up in the car and caught, in the distance, the figure of a small boy walking slowly up the sidewalk toward me. He was dressed quite formally for the heat, in long shorts and a white shirt whose short, wide sleeves only emphasized the thinness of his arms. The purpose with which he walked—leaning slightly forward from the waist—made me think that he was small for his age, for he looked to be no more than about five, but even with the distance I could make out the furrow in his brow. His black hair kept falling into his face as he walked and now and then he swept it away angrily with one hand. I watched him, barely able to move. As he approached the house, he slowed. He stopped at the sidewalk in front of the house. He turned and looked at me. I sat very still. A minute passed, maybe two. Then he took his gaze away and started walking again, past the house, up the street and I followed him with my eyes. When his tiny figure turned in the distance and vanished, I rolled up my window and drove away from the house.

The next morning, I retrieved Teresa's package from the back of the closet. I cut the twine and peeled away the tape. I emptied the box onto the table, letting the notes and photographs spill out. Slowly, I reread her story. In the days that followed, I sat for hours studying the handwriting, trying to place a date. I repaired a few of the photographs. I studied his mouth, his hands, I traced the curve of his eyes. All this I did with a cool remove, as if the story contained there were not my own, as if Teresa's notes held only a stranger's recollections, some so intimate that I turned again in modesty from their telling. But before long, the cadence of her voice began to invade my dreams. Her impossible life began to seem more real to me than my own. So it was that some weeks after receiving Teresa's package, I allowed myself the little hope that my mother had sent me a love letter. And I longed, in spite of the better judgment I had shown at the start, to prove that her words were true.

The first thing I did was send a few excerpts of Teresa's story to Dr. Caraballo, a professor of Cuban history at the University of Miami from whom I had taken some classes. Afraid that she would not remember me, I sent her a long letter explaining who I was and why I needed her help. After a few days, I received a call from her secretary asking me to send more. This I did, and after a few weeks I received a short, though thoughtful letter from the professor. She began by saying she had enjoyed the letters and had even shown them to a few colleagues, who had remarked that much of the dialogue attributed to Che could, in fact, be found in his writings—albeit, she added, in a slightly different context. She had been most intrigued, Dr. Caraballo wrote, with the background that I had included in my letter. The bit of poetry that had been pinned to my sweater had come from a poem of Pablo Neruda's, "Letter on the Road." The poem appeared in a collection that came to be known as *The Captain's Verses*. Neruda first published these poems anonymously in 1952, Dr. Caraballo wrote, but didn't acknowledge them as his own until 1963, which, if I'm correct, was a year or two after you were born. It is possible, she wrote, that whoever sent you to the United States had somehow gotten a copy of the 1952 edition published in Naples and had no idea of the authorship, only enjoyed the poem. Another, more remote explanation exists, the professor wrote. Che Guevara was a friend of the poet's, and it is conceivable that Neruda had shared these love poems with him. From that we would have to make a series of leaps to bring us to the little lines pinned onto your sweater. But it is intriguing, she wrote. And the one detail that shakes my certainty that the story this woman has written is mostly the work of imagination.

Dr. Caraballo ended her letter by inviting me to make an appointment sometime after the semester, when she would have more time to discuss these matters with me. The writings had intrigued her, she added. And she would be delighted to see me after all these years.

I put Dr. Caraballo's letter away for some days, and, in the meantime tried to, as the Cubans say, make memory, about who my mother could be.

De la Landre was not my grandfather's name, and I could not find it in the Miami phone directory, which in itself was a bad sign. I was under the impression that every Cuban exile, no matter where they may have eventually settled in the world, retained some roots in Miami. Looking up Landre in the dictionary, I found that in addition to 'hidden pocket,' the word could also mean 'swollen gland,' and I wondered if Teresa had meant this as a joke on her linguist husband. I wrote some letters to the linguistics departments at both the University of Miami and Florida International University on the remote chance that someone may have known of Calixto in Havana. I received, from FIU, a short letter telling me they could not be of help, since what I was asking was, in essence, personal information. I never got a letter from the University of Miami.

And so I tried to think back to those many trips that I had made to Havana beginning all those years before. I realized now that I should have kept a diary and taken down the name and address of everyone to whom I gave my own name and address. It was an oversight in my otherwise careful planning, and it suddenly struck me as the kind of catastrophic mistake that people who are destined for mediocrity tend to make. I cursed myself, too, because this inability to keep a diary has always vexed me. Why, I suddenly wondered, did I delight in the photographs of strangers in my travels, instead of recording my own thoughts and impressions?

Yet, for all the setbacks, the project had invested me with new vigor. I was thrilled to get up in the morning and was able for the first time in my life to work all day and into the night without tiring. It occurred to me that I was experiencing, perhaps for the first time, something like the passion that had so gripped Teresa, this unknown woman who more and more I was coming to genuinely think of as a newly discovered part of myself.

I gave myself over to the research, eventually collecting two shelves' worth of books on Che Guevara and Cuban history. I searched the Internet late into the early morning, locating first a photo of the destruction of the offices of *El Tiempo* and then several photographs of El Encanto branches all over Cuba. These last I printed out on special paper and framed. Sometimes, I like to imagine Teresa standing there, just beyond the photograph's blind edge.

Some months into my search, I made several appointments to talk to people who might have known Che Guevara well enough to give me the kinds of clues and insights that are often missing from books.

Through some old contacts from the failed photography project, I was led to Jacinto Alcazar, a onetime photographer who had fought alongside Fidel and Che and was now an old man. When I called him, he seemed eager to meet me and suggested that I go immediately to his apartment, that very afternoon. Instead, I made an appointment to see him two days

later. He sounded disappointed, but then cheered while giving me the somewhat complicated directions to his place.

He lived in a complex of apartment buildings that took
up several blocks and that one could enter from various different directions. After some confusion, I succeeded in finding the entrance he had told me about, which was guarded by
a mechanical arm and a tiny old woman in a white booth. I
gave her my name and the name of the man I was seeing, and
she dialed him. After a moment, the mechanical arm rose with
a lurch, and I wasted some more minutes driving aimlessly in
the vast parking lot beyond it.

When finally I found Jacinto's building (as I recall they
were designated by number and letter), I was mildly exhausted.
I paused for a few moments to catch my breath in the deserted
lobby before riding the elevator to the fourth floor.

I found him waiting for me in the hallway, walking up
and down the dim corridor. He wanted to know if I had gotten lost and seemed very anxious about the directions he had
given me. I followed him inside the apartment, all the time
reassuring him that I'd found him with no trouble at all. The
apartment was small, and was made even smaller by the
books and papers that were crammed everywhere. In contrast to some others I had seen in my searching, though,
Jacinto's apartment was clean, and after a while I came to
see the space as almost cheerful. Too many people my age, it
occurred to me, had so streamlined their apartments that
they had, in their neuroses, removed every trace of human-
ity from between their four walls.

Jacinto led me to a small study, also crammed with books, but with a large window that afforded an expansive view of the outside world, though most of it consisted of the parking lot. A woman that I didn't see again brought a plate of cookies and glasses of water.

Not knowing Jacinto, I had been reluctant to give him a copy of Teresa's story. Instead, after the usual pleasantries, I told him that I was doing some writings on the revolution and that a mutual acquaintance had suggested that he could tell me some good stories about that time.

He launched then into a long discussion that I could barely keep up with in my notebook. Yes, he had been at the presidential palace shortly after Echeverría was shot; no, he didn't remember pigeons in the plaza, and why would I ask about something like that? Yes, he had fought first in the cities with the Revolutionary Student Directorate and then had gone into the mountains to fight with the scraggly band of rebels after their shipwreck. Yes, he had believed that what he was doing was right and important. He talked for a long time and after a while his story began to come apart, jumping as it did from one subject to another, one time to another, one place to another according to a narrative that made sense only to him, as if the past and the present were only different countries that one might visit at will. Several times I tried to steer him back to the conversation and once or twice he told me a truly moving anecdote. He had been, he said in one of these thoughtful, calmer moments, with Fidel on the road from Santiago to Bayamo after the first days of the triumph. All the men were walking alongside him. The crowds, Jacinto said, lined the road for miles. It was the most astonishing thing I had ever seen, he said. I was riding just behind Fidel on top of a tank and we were all waving to the crowds and as the tank proceeded slowly, almost at a walking pace, we could hear what the people were saying to us. All up and down that road, Jacinto said, the people shouted for Fidel. Fidel, you are our savior. Fidel, this is your house. Thank you, Fidel. Fidel, our redeemer. By the time we reached Bayamo I noted, for the first time, a change in Fidel. I am convinced that it was on that day he began to believe those things about himself. Before that time I believed he was sincere about democracy and the people. But after that day, I saw how much he had enjoyed this welcome, appropriate to kings and gods, and that it was inevitable that it would change him profoundly.

Jacinto sat in contemplation for a while and then he said, Do you know that poem of Lorca, *When the full moon breaks, I shall go to Santiago de Cuba, I shall go to Santiago in a coach of black waters?* I always think of that poem when I tell this story. He laughed. I always liked Lorca, even after I stopped being a communist.

I smiled. What can you tell me about the newspaper *El Tiempo?* I asked him. He thought for a moment, his face registering what I took to be the rusty workings of his memory, until he brightened and said, Masferrer's paper. Yes, he said, it was completely trashed after the revolution. Later it was said that he had filled the paper with lies and calumnies. And it's true that many people found him disagreeable; I myself never knew him. Certainly the paper had a reputation for inciting passions.

But you know, nothing really died in the revolution, he said with a smile. Havana's pathologies and beauties came to splendor in Miami. Sometimes I think this exile has been little more than a brief passage through a mirror. And so the owner of *El Tiempo* ended up publishing another little sheet in Miami. Did you know this? I shook my head. I think, Jacinto said, that it was called *Libertad;* we moved from time to liberty and back again. Anyway, he continued, maybe you are too young to remember this: In late October of 1975, I think it was, he wrote an editorial in favor of political bombings. A few days later, he was killed when his car blew up.

Before I left, I found the courage to ask Jacinto what he could tell me about Che, specifically any love affairs he had had. This last question seemed to cheer him immensely, and his eyebrows darted up lasciviously. Ah! So this is what this is about. He laughed for a long time and then he stood with some difficulty and disappeared into another room. He returned with a packet of typed copies of some writings in Spanish. I looked them over quickly. One seemed of particular interest, a letter that purported to be from René Ramos Latour "to Che Guevara from Santiago de Cuba 18 December of 1957." Later, at home, I read it more closely. I reproduce part of it here only because its lines seem to mirror so closely the pleadings of a spurned lover, and reading them I always feel a pang for Teresa, as if the ghost of her betrayal was already hovering about Che's dealings with those who were closest to him.

Che, Latour writes, I have just received in my hands the letter that you yourself have described as "difficult" and whose contents, to put it plainly, surprise me even as they in no way have the power to hurt me, for I am very far from considering myself a traitor to the Cuban Revolution and remain so deeply satisfied with my short, but pure and honorable, revolutionary life that I will never be wounded by the words of those who, as yourself, do not know me well enough to judge me.

Jacinto insisted on walking me to my car, and when I closed the door and waved to him, he tapped on the windshield to signal me to lower it. I'll tell you two things about El Che, he said into the car: The man didn't like to shower. Despite this, when he was in the Sierra, he was able to take for a lover the most delicious little mulata in the whole of Oriente.

I next went to see Ileana, an aficionado of Cuban art, whom I knew through mutual friends. I hoped that she might have heard of an artist named Teresa who lived in El Vedado after the revolution. And if de La Landre wasn't her real name, I hoped at least that Ileana would be able to give me some clues as to who she might have been.

Ileana was working then at Vizcaya as a consultant to the curator. I sent ahead the parts of Teresa's story that I thought would most interest her and arranged to meet her at the museum the following Tuesday.

In her office, which wasn't in the main house but in a temporary trailer just outside the grounds by the service gate, Ileana told me that she had been intrigued by the excerpts of Teresa's story and was curious about the rest. She then pulled out some notes that she had taken. Unfortunately, she told me up front, she had no knowledge of an artist named Teresa working during those years. She had also made some inquiries with contacts in Cuba and though they were still asking around, they did not have any recollection that might be helpful to me. But this, she told me, did not mean very much. The times were very chaotic then, she reminded me, and many galleries and collectors had run into difficulties. Many of the capital's wealthiest collectors were often in a rush to leave, some afraid for their lives. As you may know, Ileana said, many hid their art behind walls. In other cases, some very fine collections were confiscated by the state. It was quite conceivable that an artist, even a very good one, could have been working in obscurity during those turbulent times, might even prefer to be working in obscurity.

She launched then into an account of her own education and her thoughts on Cuban art. The forties and fifties, she said, had given rise to one of the most exciting periods in Cuban modernism, as if all the turbulence of those years had been compressed and reinterpreted in lush palettes. This was the time of the greats: Wifredo Lam, Victor Manuel, Rene Portocarrero. There was also a woman, very well known at the time, named Amelia Pelaez. Ileana must have seen my expression change because she quickly added, But this couldn't have been your Teresa—I believe Amelia was into her sixties by the time of the revolution, and anyway, she died in Havana in 1968. After a while, she continued, Amelia is a favorite of mine. She was born in my home province of Las Villas and when her family moved to Havana they settled in La Vibora, which is where my own family eventually settled. Perhaps we formed similar impressions of the world—or perhaps, Ileana said laughing, I'm flattering myself. No matter how hard we try to be objective and scholarly about art, one's favorite artists always end up saying more about one's own world than anything else. A friend of mine, she said, a melancholy sort, has long been obsessed with a painting by a Belgian contemporary of Rembrandt's named Michael Sweerts. The painting, *Burying the Dead,* has never appealed to me—I think it's static and gloomy in a rather melodramatic way—but to him it speaks to all our anxieties about death, and into the distant building he reads the classicism of Rome that might yet comfort us. Me, she said, I've never believed that redemption lies in the past. Ileana smiled.

Anyway, she continued, Amelia is a favorite of mine precisely because she was part of the movement then that was breaking with the past. Here Ileana stood and walked to her small bookcase. She took down a book, flipped through the pages and then held it out to me. I turned through the pages for a while. You can see the cubist influence, certainly, she said. But there is something else, an exuberance, that to me has always seemed particularly Cuban, even in our darkest times.

Amelia, incidentally, designed the plates at El Gato Tuerto, the legendary Havana nightclub where artists used to gather. I don't know if it's still there, Ileana continued. Are you planning to go to Havana? I would think you are. Maybe you can ask there. If you go, you should also visit the great artists' studio near the cathedral. It was opened in the early 1960s when Pablo Neruda persuaded his friend Che Guevara to provide presses and a studio for a group of printmakers. It's very easy to find; you can't miss it.

Ileana then drew me a little map and wrote down a name. If you go to Havana, you should get in touch with this man who runs the studio. Mention my name, she said; he's a friend. I always buy a few pieces from him when I'm there. Ileana talked a little bit more about the contemporary arts scene in Havana and then asked me if I would like a tour of the museum and the grounds. Having nothing else planned for the day and genuinely charmed by Ileana, I gladly accepted.

After my visit to Ileana, I began to consider her suggestion to travel to Cuba again. She had mentioned it in such a casual way that I felt a fool for not thinking of it myself. Often I wondered if it was really necessary for me to press forward with these desultory investigations into Teresa's life. But I had embarked on a quest that I now had to see through to its finish. And finally I knew that I must travel to Cuba again.

* * *

Before I left, I called Dr. Caraballo and reminded the secretary of the professor's offer to see me.

She received me some days later in her office, which was small but bright and decorated with framed cigar box covers. I found her tall and elegant and was surprised at how little I remembered of her. As she spoke, I noticed that she was studying my face as well. Still holding my hand, she led me to a chair and then sat down at her desk. The shelves behind her were stacked with books, every one of them, as far as I could tell, about Cuba. One long case held rows and rows of novels. The other two were crammed with history books, quite a few of which I recognized from my own growing collection.

A little disconcerting, isn't it, she said, following my gaze. One feels instinctively that they can't all be right.

I smiled at this. I was very happy to hear from you, Dr. Caraballo said. Of course I remembered you, or I should say I remembered your work. You were doing something on the writings of Martí, weren't you? I nodded. How he had invented the concept of the Cuban exile? She nodded back and then reached under some magazines to pull out a file. She began to go through the papers that I recognized as Teresa's story. I was very interested in this when you first sent it, she said. She looked up at me and was quiet for a while, and this time I had to look away from her gaze. I was quite interested, she continued after a time, because any new information on Che Guevara's life is, of course, of immediate interest. He is probably the best-known Cuban in the world after Fidel, which should tell you something—our best-known Cuban turned out to be an egomaniac and our second-best-known Cuban was a foreigner. Is it any wonder we make such exemplary exiles?

She leaned back in her chair, laughing at her joke. When she had calmed, she shook her head and said, Well. I took a special interest, too, because I came to this country by myself when I was sixteen years old. Here Dr. Caraballo paused to look at me again, and I couldn't decide if it was my features that interested her or if she was trying to read some lie in my face. I lived in Indiana for some months, she continued, still studying me. It was fine until winter arrived. It wasn't just the cold, which was bad enough, but the darkness, that afternoon gloom of which we are completely ignorant in the tropics.

She paused for a time before continuing. I was reunited with my parents the following year and we moved to Miami. But I think I can understand that feeling of vastness at your back that you described in your letter. I can understand how in the absence of a past, one might be tempted to invent history. Dr. Caraballo looked at me very closely. In this sense, I cannot agree with your Teresa when she likens history to personal events. The world is much bigger than ourselves, though it is pleasant to think it might fit in the space of our fist.

I wondered if she was accusing me of having written Teresa's account myself, but not wishing to seem paranoid and thereby magnify the perception of guilt, I only nodded as if I agreed. I expected Dr. Caraballo to continue, but she sat looking at me with a curious expression. I was then at a loss and, my usual shyness overtaking me, I mumbled some thanks and asked if there had been a specific reason she had wanted to see me, other than to extend her kindness, which she had done and which I was grateful for.

Well, Dr. Caraballo began, I wanted to see you, of course. And also, I didn't want to disappoint you in a letter. You were a very good student, as I recall, your research always impeccable. She leaned forward on her desk. Perhaps you know that a woman named Lilia Rosa Perez gave birth to a child of Che's in the early sixties, 1963 or 1964. Dr. Caraballo paused, and I could tell she was waiting for a reaction to show itself across my face. No, I said, I didn't know that. Dr. Caraballo nodded. The child was a boy, she said. You know, Lilia had met Che in Santa Clara—I think that would have been 1958—and then again at La Cabaña. You have to admit, she said, that La Cabaña is a likelier place than El Vedado to make the acquaintance of a revolutionary.

I leaned back in my chair. You are saying the story is a lie? I said. Dr. Caraballo shrugged and said, Does it matter to you? I didn't respond. There are some errors in the dates, she said. Omissions. Maybe this isn't important to a love story. I don't know. Myself, she said smiling, I would have liked to have seen something about how we have Mr. Guevara to thank for introducing Soviet-style prisons to Cuba. I'm sorry, Dr. Caraballo continued, more serious, I'm not here to dash whatever hopes you had. I don't know anything about you. But it was difficult for me to read about that man as a lover; it was difficult to see his photograph. I wanted to help you in any way I could, but if you really want my opinion, I'm afraid that what you have here is an impossible reinvention of history, a beautiful fraud.

I was quiet. After a moment, she stood and I stood also. She walked to me and looked at my face again for a long time and then, to my shock, she reached over and ran her fingers over my forehead. Your forehead protrudes, she said softly. And I, beginning to sweat, thanked her again and, wishing to save her dignity as well as my own, walked out as quickly as I decently could.

So often in Miami I have departed from a friendly conversation with a lingering chill, as if some malignancy ran beneath the surface. So often, as I did with Dr. Caraballo, I had the sense that the person chatting so pleasantly with me was only waiting to be offended, to detect in some innocent or ignorant statement a secret adherence to repellent beliefs.

Perhaps what unsettled me was the suspicion that the professor might be right; that Teresa's story was impossible. My plans already set, however, I had little choice but to depart for Cuba a few days later.

On Ileana's suggestion, I had applied for a visa to travel legally to the island, something I had never bothered with before. As family, I listed "Teresa de la Landre, address unknown." And to my surprise, the visa was granted.

I was to travel by charter flight from Miami to Havana and was advised to be at the airport at least four hours before the scheduled departure time. I took a cab to Miami International and when the driver asked me where I was traveling, I told him, without thinking, Havana. I watched his face change shape in the rearview mirror and sat still as he went on a tirade about giving money to Castro. I explained that I didn't plan to spend very much, that I wasn't a tourist and that I was only trying to find my mother. This last mention seemed to calm him, and after a while he said in a softer voice, This has been the worst legacy of the Cuban Revolution, this tearing apart of families. His own son, he said, was still in Cuba with his mother. He hadn't seen him in fourteen years. When I got off, the driver helped me with my luggage and kissed me farewell on the cheek.

Inside the terminal to which I'd been directed by the agency, I found no evidence of a flight to Cuba. Everyone I asked, from porters to ticket agents, looked me up and down before answering that they had no idea. I felt, after a while, as if I were asking for directions to the nearest porn emporium.

After a few anxious minutes of wandering around the concourse, I spotted some stairs and decided I had nothing to lose by descending. It was so dark that at first I could barely make out the throngs of people standing in line below.

Over the next several hours, the line shifted, bulged, thinned, but never seemed to move. People came and went as if they had been standing there simply for the experience. The whole thing had such an air of unreality that I began to wonder if I had lost my mind. Then, just one hour before the flight was scheduled to depart, the line acquired a sudden orderliness, and it occurred to me that most of these people were used to the drill. My anxiety gone, I could now concentrate on the conversations around me. In front of me stood a group of trim and distinguished older people who I came to decide were professors. One appeared drunk, though not vulgarly so. She was the most animated of the group, and I couldn't help staring at her as she excitedly discussed all the fabulous places they would see, the fabulous architecture and the fabulous people. There then ensued a discussion of the ingredients of a *mojito,* which I felt tempted to enter into before thinking better of it.

Behind me stood a dour couple with a young boy I took to be their son. The three were dressed in very new and very bright clothing, and I decided that they were Cubans returning from a visit with their Miami relatives. They didn't talk very much and when they did it was in barely audible whispers. Like most of the other travelers, they were burdened with large and obviously heavy bags. But theirs had been wrapped in plastic by those semi-hucksters who've proliferated across airports in the last years.

These sealed shabby bags, looking rather like shrink-wrapped rags, attracted the attention of the professors. They discussed the odd-looking bags among themselves for a moment before one of them stepped forward to ask the family outright why they had wrapped their bags in plastic. The man shook his head to indicate that he didn't understand, so the happy professor asked him in Spanish. The man looked at his wife and she shook her head and whispered something, holding her son very close to her. The man shrugged and shook his head. No reason, he said in English. The woman insisted, But I just don't understand. What is the purpose? No purpose, the man said, no reason, no problem. The woman began to insist again and the man behind me simply turned his back and began to talk to his wife in a low voice. I couldn't even be sure what language they were speaking.

By this time, the scheduled departure time of the flight had come and gone. But strangely, my usual anxiety was absent. I felt part of a flowing mass of people that seemed stronger than schedules. Presently, I came to a woman at a foldout table who checked my name, passport and visa number against a computer printout. After this I was given a number and, after another wait, was finally allowed to pass into another chamber with my baggage, where several guards picked up our bags, poking them here and there, before depositing them on a conveyor belt that then sent them through a huge white contraption that looked like an MRI machine. By the time I emerged from the underground darkness, holding my ticket, I was recalling with fondness how easy it had been to travel through Jamaica all those years before. I was beginning to regret this form of legal travel and dreading whatever sister-tortures awaited me on the other side in Havana. It was now two hours past the departure time, but when I asked a woman at the gate about it, she just smiled and said, Don't worry so much.

In Havana, it was past midnight by the time we made it off the airplane and onto a rickety bus that deposited us at the terminal. My heart sank a little at the seemingly interminable line at immigration. But this moved fairly quickly.

And the young and nice-looking man who took down my information ended by asking me for a date. Past immigration, the airport was empty, most of the lights out. We gathered our bags, and I was surprised and relieved to find that no one was guarding the exit.

Though it was, I believe, a weeknight, the crowds were five or six deep outside the airport. Most of the men and women seemed to be shouting for relatives, many of whom I imagined might have changed over the years to the point of being unrecognizable. I took a rattling car to the Habana Libre, scarcely aware of the dark countryside around me; at the hotel, I handed my voucher to the woman at the reception desk and barely made it up to my room before collapsing into bed.

I was woken very early the next morning by the sun coming in through the open blinds. It took me a few seconds to remember where I was. I walked to the window and stood in front of it for some moments.

I had been given a high, ocean-facing room and the water took up almost half the view. It shone silver and blue in the early light, and my throat seized at the beauty of it. I knew, too, that beyond the line where the ocean seemed to meet the sky lay Miami, that short, short flight away that somehow now seemed the longest flight I had taken in my life, so far away did I suddenly feel from that world I had left. To the west, the proud lines of the Nacional Hotel. And below me, around me, the streets of Havana, just now beginning to fill with life. I

looked over the city, amazed, as one tends to be when viewing the streets from this distance, at how small and tidy it all
seemed. My eyes fell over the small row houses to the east,
and I wondered from which one Teresa had made her dreams.
Upon which balcony did she stand to stare up at the hotel
where I now stood at the window, as if I were looking down
into the eyes of my own past?

I was thinking these things in a sort of dream state when I
gradually became aware of a low droning noise. I turned my
gaze here and there until finally from behind a building there
emerged, as if torn from another dimension, an old biplane.
It passed low and so close to the window that I thought I had
a view of the pilot before I snapped out of my shock and ducked
down to the ground. I sat crouched below the window until
the droning noise faded and then I stood, suddenly very awake,
and wondering if I had invented this vision. A few moments
later, I heard the droning again and the plane emerged from
behind the hotel, this time with its pilot waving, I thought, in
my direction.

I don't usually take breakfast in hotels, preferring to find a small
cafe where I can linger over coffee in silence without the agi-
tation brought on by large families, who seem, by some uni-
versal law of travel, to breakfast exclusively in hotel cafeterias.
But from what I remembered of Havana, the cafe option was
out. So I took the elevator down to the dining room with trepi-
dation, not only over the noise of unruly travel-exhausted chil-

dren that surely awaited me, but over the dreadful food that
had no doubt been laid out with heartbreaking ceremony.
When last I had been here, the country was beginning its slide
into the special period and even tourists—those revered dei-
ties of the tropics—had to make due with white toast and a
revolting gray lunch meat served day after day in a dingy dining room.

Downstairs, I was greeted with much attention by an
eager and aggressive klatch of waiters. One took my breakfast voucher (Havana, it seemed, had moved to the dollar and
voucher economy), another checked my name on a computer
and a third finally smiled and pointed me to the main room.

There, I was amazed to find not the sad state that I had
remembered, not even the sorry buffet one encounters now
and then in the lesser hotels of Europe, but a gleaming dining
room arranged around islands piled high with tropical fruits,
several kinds of breads, pastries, juices and real bacon and
sausages. At one end, a woman in a black and white uniform
poured out guava juice into small glasses. At the other, a jovial
man in a tall white hat took orders for omelets. I stood in
the omelet line, and after I told the cook what I wanted he
asked me where I was from. Not wanting to attract attention to myself as an American, I answered, almost without
thinking, Spain. He looked at me for a second and said, Ah,
the south, then. I nodded, and was distressed when he kept
asking me questions. When did I arrive? Just last night. Alone?
Was this man working for the government? I couldn't decide if I was paranoid or tired, but just the same, I answered

that I was alone at the moment but my husband would join me shortly.

Later, relaxing with my second cup of coffee, I wondered where that response about a husband had come from. I had never been self-conscious about being unmarried. And I didn't think that I was self-conscious now. The fact that I had not yet married was one of those things that I accepted. I didn't feel much about it either way. I had nothing against the idea of marriage, just as I didn't expect that being married would change my life in any significant way. I had been in love a few times and it had been pleasant, but it had never been the way one saw in movies, the way Teresa had written about it. I had no way of knowing, of course, if this was failure on my part or the world's; in the end each of us exists in a small universe of our own making. But now, this outburst about a husband made me wonder just how certain I could be about the things I believed.

I made a left out of the hotel and walked toward L Street, the neighborhood still familiar to me after all those trips to my grandfather's old streets. I knew she no longer lived at the old house, but I suppose that I still hoped I might be able to find someone who knew her. I didn't have a plan on how I would find her. And I had already considered the likelihood that she didn't want me to find her. After all, if what she wrote was true, she had had her chance some years before to engage me in person and had chosen instead to send me an anonymous packet. And she had never included her address.

I walked down L for a while and then turned on 25th and followed this toward the water. I was reminded of all those years past when I had walked along some of these same streets with much the same goal: to learn of my parents. Then, it had not seemed so daunting to knock on the doors of strangers. But in the time that had passed, my natural shyness must have settled into me, rather like a stain setting with age, and several times on that final trip back to Havana I turned away from a door, my hands sweating. I knew that eventually I would have to do it, would have to knock on a stranger's door and ask questions and be engaged. But that first day I decided to give myself more time to get used to the idea. And so I spent my first hours in Havana acting like any other tourist, stopping now and then in front of a crumbling old beautiful house to admire its lines, all the while wondering, Is this the one?

Thinking back on this, I believe I was also thrown by how much the city had changed in ten years, how little it resembled the Havana I remembered. Dollars, which were still illegal when I first began coming here, were now the only accepted currency in most places. The entrance around even the smallest hotels swarmed with beautiful young women in short skirts, special companions to the European tourists who had turned the clock back on the capital. Watching one long-legged beauty on the arm of a round little man, I wondered how many of these tourists claimed sympathy to the revolution even as they savored the fruits that Batista had once tended so well.

Everywhere, the socialist experiment seemed dead and buried, awaiting only the death and burial of its maximum

leader. The men and women I passed in the streets were better dressed than I remembered, all of them moving quickly as if
in a great hurry to get somewhere. And on every other block I
discovered a new store. I wandered in and out of these, hoping
to find some old photographs or books. But most seemed dedi-
cated to the most basic kinds of longings. At street level under
the hotel, several stores had opened, including a liquor store with
wine and champagne and bright red boxes of Pringles. The Focsa,
a dismal apartment complex that I remembered stumbling upon
during my last visit, now bustled with stores, and even a kiosk
to check purses and bags. I walked through the dark little maze
under the building until I came upon a dollar store, not in the
old Cuban tradition of diplo-tiendas, but a dollar store as de-
fined by Miami: a little hole-in-the-wall, selling every manner
of cheap trinket for an American dollar. More incredible was
the line of people waiting to get inside.

That evening, I walked to El Nacional for a drink and to
write my notes. I sat outside on the porch overlooking the sea.
Passing on the mojito that the waiter tried to force on me, I
ordered instead a glass of white wine. I sat drinking it, lulled
by the breeze and the easy beauty of the hotel, the lawn, the
people; and when I was done I ordered another glass. And then
surprised myself by ordering a third. The wine hit me pretty
hard and I sat out until it was dark, trying to gather my senses.

I slept badly, blaming it on the wine. Sometime in the night I
woke, sure that I had heard the wind banging. But when I

opened the blinds, the scene before me was serene; the moonlight reflected smoothly on the water. I returned to bed, still
unsettled. Suddenly everything about the trip seemed wrong,
the task before me impossible.

Morning found me in a better state, though I rose with the
unhappy feeling that something terrible had happened. At breakfast, the omelet man greeted me as La Española, and I took a
table in the farthest corner of the room to avoid his gaze. I was
determined that day to knock on a few doors. But first I thought
I would take a walk to find my courage. This time, once out of
the hotel and onto 25th, I decided to walk away from the water.
I passed a church and, peering in, realized it was Sunday, the
pews packed with worshipers. I walked on. I turned at a corner, and after a few more blocks a little boy fell in step with me
and together we walked in silence. Hello, I finally said in English. Hello, he answered back. Are you British? I thought for a
moment. Cuban, I said. He stopped dead, feigning great surprise, and I laughed at this hard little actor. For a long stretch
the little boy walked with me, pointing out houses and telling
me fantastical stories about them: And that house there is where
a famous dragon used to live. See where it's burned by his breath?
That's where he stood every day to watch the people pass. The
child was delightful, and I found myself after a while following
him instead of him me. We came, or he led me, finally to a sprawl-
ing open-air market that seemed to rise as a mirage out of a
colorless little part of Havana. Before I could protest much, he
had grabbed me by the hand and led me in. We passed kiosks
piled high with heads of lettuce, carrots, radishes, tomatoes, piles

and piles of fresh greens. The little boy, whose name I still didn't know, pulled me along until he finally stopped in front of a display of meat and began to order. I played the dupe and we spent the next hour or so shopping like mother and son, he devising the menu and I supplying the dollars, which along with something called the dollar peso seemed to be the only currency accepted.

We left the open market burdened with bags. I followed the boy through twists and turns of streets and cracked sidewalks and old men who stood to watch us go by. We arrived after what seemed an interminable walk at a large block of apartment buildings. My feet throbbed and my fingers were red and sore where the bags hung. The little boy invited me up to see his mother, but I politely refused. I was still a little wary of entering people's homes, a habit of many travels in solitude. The boy insisted and when I made it clear that I wouldn't budge he began to call up to the windows, Oye, Vieja! Vieja!

After a few seconds of this, a beautiful young woman appeared at one of the sixth-floor windows and waved, making hand signals to come up. At last, I relented, following the boy through a front door that, though its glass front was completely gone, he insisted on opening for me.

I stood then at the bottom of a grimy box-way of stairs, the boy already racing ahead of me. I was so exhausted from the walk to whatever part of town I now found myself in that the climb took me several long minutes, and by the time I made it to the apartment the boy's mother was apologizing, saying everyone experienced difficulties with the stairs, but that she and the boy were so used to them that they barely noticed. Eventually, one adapts to almost anything and stops complaining, the woman said. She laughed, looking me over, and then added, That's why this country is in the state it's in.

I followed the woman and the boy into the apartment. It consisted of just two rooms set apart by a gas burner. But it was neat and bright. The young woman sat me down on a sofa and brought me coffee, all the while talking almost too quickly for me to follow. She didn't apologize for the boy's corralling me into buying all that food, but she thanked me so profusely that I took it she and the charming boy had developed a good scam, part of whose successful execution was to pretend that the victim was just a generous visitor arriving for an appointed lunch.

The woman, who had introduced herself as Judi, cooked furiously at the little stove as she talked. Forget education and equality and health care, she said, Without dollars in this country you're as good as dead. Which means you might as well bury yourself under a sidewalk at the Colon cemetery if you don't have family in Miami, if you don't know anybody in the counterrevolutionary Miami Mafia—and this last part she said with such a deep, brilliant imitation of Castro, complete with upraised finger, that I laughed. You look to me like a professional, Judi continued without letting me answer. You probably go to an office in the day, pay bills, see friends. Do you have any idea of the boredom we endure here? There's no police state here; that would at least be exciting. No, the police can't follow you around—once you got into a car, you'd leave their bicycles in the dust. Instead, they have anesthetized us with boredom. Cuban days are the longest in all the world. Even work, such as it is, is boring. You could disappear for three months and no one would notice. All these new clubs and stores around here, do you think any Cuban can afford them? She let out an exaggerated sigh. Our entertainment consists of figuring out how to get enough food for dinner. She waited a beat before adding, And even this is boring. Judi continued in this vein for a while, her observations becoming more and more outrageous until I began to suspect that she was giving me a rather cartoon version of what she expected I wanted to hear, perhaps her way of paying me for my attention and generosity. I finally decided that her true thoughts were private and unknowable.

As she talked, I was quiet, not able to get one word in and also mesmerized by the volume of food that she was managing to furiously put together on her little stove. Little by little, as she talked, new dishes emerged, which she handed to her son without hesitating a second in her narrative. The rickety card table where the boy laid the dishes quickly was becoming crowded with salads and rice and black beans and stewed radishes and beets.

Over lunch, Judi became more serious, as if her story could afford to slow down now that she was finished with her manic cooking. She was only looking for the opportunity to leave, she said, though she'd never be so stupid as to take this poor innocent child on a raft. Thank God, she said, the rafter business had died down. Now and then, the Cuban wakes up for a little bit, Judi said, and it's like a sudden fever, all of a

sudden everyone has to get out. It's a kind of panic, as if someone had just yelled Fire! in a building. During the last rafter
crisis, Judi said, I thought that I alone would be left in Havana.
One morning, I passed by the statue of Martí in the park, and
you know what they had done to him? Judi laughed. These
Cubans, she said. From his outstretched arm, someone had
carefully hung a large suitcase.

I parted from Judi and the boy with promises to return, though
we all knew I probably wouldn't. Walking away from the building, I wondered how many other tourists had fallen for their
delightful little game.

I found my way back to the hotel by asking people to point
me in the direction of the malecón (a system I developed after
a surprising number seemed to have no idea what the Habana
Libre was) until I saw the top of the hotel rising over the rooftops. This first accidental interview had gone so pleasantly that
I was emboldened to consider knocking on some doors. But
by the time I returned to the hotel more than an hour later,
the courage had drained out of me. I was also exhausted. So,
promising myself that I would begin tomorrow first thing in
the morning, I took the elevator to my room and fell asleep
almost instantly, satiated and happy.

The following morning, I awoke full of energy, and wishing
to avoid the omelet man, I decided to skip breakfast and get

right to work. I took the usual left out of the hotel and began once more to walk the streets of El Vedado. I was wandering about talking to myself and trying to decide where I should start when I found myself in front of a pastry store, Pain de Paris. The store was narrow and deep and one entire wall was taken up by glass display cases that held every kind of French delicacy: pink and blue petits fours, tiny fruit tarts, rows of baguettes. When the door shut behind me, blocking out the din of the city, and the smell of the place overtook me, I had the sudden unshakable feeling that the previous days had been a dream and I was just now sitting down to breakfast at the little cafe near the Place de la Concorde. I ordered a palmier and sat facing the street, hoping to force my mind around the incongruity of this place's existing in these streets.

The sky soon clouded over; it looked like rain. Instead of cursing the weather, I was suddenly grateful for something that would finally persuade me to take refuge inside someone's house. I left the cafe and crossed the street, and after stalling for a few minutes, trying to decide between a blue house or a gray one, I finally stepped up to the heavy door of a third house and knocked hard. I waited several long minutes. No one answered. I stepped back into the street and looked up; all the blinds were drawn and, in fact, the house looked deserted. Turning, I caught the eye of a woman looking at me from a high balcony in a house across the street. She waved over and I waved back. After a few seconds of this, she shouted for me to come in out of the rain.

I called up a quick thanks and she disappeared inside. I walked to the door and waited. After a moment, the door popped open and I was surprised to find no one waiting behind it, just a steep climb of stairs. It was then that I noted the rope that had been strung from the top of the stairs down to the door lock. The woman waited at the top with one end of the rope in her hands. To my astonishment, she was in a wheelchair. Make sure you shut the door well behind you, she said.

When I reached the top she nodded and introduced herself as Caridad and led me into a dark but tidy reception room. The contrast with the tiny apartment I had been in the previous day was striking. Though the apartment was in need of paint and some repair, its fine lines were visible everywhere. The floor was a light tile, marred only by a few tire marks from the wheelchair. Elegant wooden screens covered the window, shielding the rooms from the sun and leaving everything in a soothing half-light. The rain fell outside, muted through the window screens.

Late summer is like this, the woman said. It can rain at any time. She excused herself and rolled out into a back room and around a corner. I spent the next few moments scanning the room: the cane-backed rocking chairs, the dark polished armoire, the bookcase full of books in French, a small gallery of photos. These last, of course, instantly interested me, and I was about to stand and look at them more closely when Caridad returned with a tray holding two small cups of coffee and a plate of cookies that I recognized from the display case at Pain de Paris.

Those are my nieces, she said, following my gaze. I've never met them; they live in Miami—my brother's children. He has a house in Coral Gables and another one in France—somewhere on the coast, I think it is. Caridad set the tray down on a table in front of me and rolled over to the desk to pick up a photo. She brought it back to me. A little girl in pigtails standing in front of what I recognized as the Fontainebleau Hotel in Miami. Do you know this hotel? I asked. Caridad shook her head. I've never been out of Cuba, she said. She put the photo down on a seat and parked her wheelchair in front of me.

She was dressed in draped black slacks and a beautiful red silk blouse that exposed her collarbone. I could tell that she had once been striking. Her nails, which I noticed when she held the plate of cookies out to me, were carefully manicured and painted a deep glossy red that matched her blouse. She took a sip of coffee and regarded me for a moment. I thanked her for the coffee and the excellent cookies.

I've been watching you walk around the streets for the last couple of days, she said. I spend a lot of time out on the balcony—it's the only time I get to spend out in the sunlight. I figured you were looking for an address, but you didn't seem like you were in a hurry, like anyone was expecting you.

She leaned back and relaxed against her wheelchair as if she were reclining on a divan. I half expected to find a highball in one of her hands and a long cigarette holder in the other. She had such a languid way about her that I had a feeling of being almost hypnotized. After some time, I noticed that she hadn't spoken in a while, and I took this to mean that she had asked a question that I hadn't heard.

I'm sorry, I said.

I was asking what it is that you're looking for, Caridad said.

I'm looking for a woman named Teresa, I said, hoping to catch a slight change in her expression that would tell me what my heart so wanted to believe: that this was the woman, that this was my mother, whom I had stumbled on so quickly and easily as if drawn by fate. But her face didn't register anything. And instead she said, Family of yours? My mother, I said. And then I added, Though I've no memory of her.

Caridad sat, reclined in her wheelchair. I see, she said.

The rain continued to fall outside.

Have you lived in this neighborhood long? I asked after a moment.

I was born in this very house, she said.

Did you ever know a woman named Teresa de la Landre? A painter? Her husband was a professor at the university. Calixto. Linguistics.

Caridad turned her eyes to the ceiling for a moment and then shook her head slowly. I know everyone who has ever passed through this neighborhood, she said. And I can tell you without any doubt that there has never been anyone by that name here.

Maybe she gave me a false name, I said.

Gave you? So you've talked with her, Caridad said.

No, not really, I said. And I began slowly to tell this stranger the story of my life.

By the time I was done, the rain outside had stopped and new sounds came up to us: the tires on the pavement, children out again and playing in puddles, their laughter coming up to us like tinkling glass.

Caridad sat for a while. I see, she said. I see.

I stood and thanked her for the coffee and cookies.

My son is at work now, she said. But he'll be here all day on Saturday. Why don't you come back for dinner.

I told her she was very kind, but that really—

Eight in the evening, she said. We'll expect you.

I walked some more of the neighborhood, stopping now and then beneath a balcony, trying to remember the one I had called up to all those years ago. When I returned to the hotel it was already getting dark. I decided to go straight to my room. I turned on the television and was startled when the image reconstituted itself on the screen and I realized I was watching CNN. So much of the last days had seemed like a dream, or like a travel in a remote universe, that the banal, inoffensive broadcast jolted me back to life. I spent the rest of the night making notes, finally falling asleep sometime past two in the morning.

I ate breakfast again at Pain de Paris, happy to be out of the hotel. I finished quickly and decided to get straight to work. The previous night I had worked out a plan that, to my surprise, was not difficult to stick to. With L as my dividing line,

I would begin on odd streets and visit every fifth house below L. The following day, I would take the even streets and do the same. The day after that, I would venture to the blocks above L. And then I would cross 23rd and do the same with the neighborhood around the Focsa.

This new plan reassured me; it seemed almost scientific, and I actually looked forward to the assignment I had given myself. The first house I knocked on was a little brown two-story row house. I knocked at the door for a long time and had begun to walk away, a little worried over my inauspicious start, when the door opened.

The woman who stood inside was very young and held a dishrag in her hand. She seemed impatient, and when I began to tell her that I was looking for a woman, an artist, named Teresa de la Landre, she immediately cut me off. I just moved in here a month ago. I'm from Güines and don't know anybody; I'm sorry. She gave me a thin smile and closed the door. I wasn't surprised. It was the treatment I had grown accustomed to in my previous visits—the same treatment I might expect anywhere in the world. I myself would never invite a stranger into my house. It was only Judi's and Caridad's hospitality that had thrown me off my original expectations.

This rejection, though, had the strange effect of encouraging me to continue; maybe I imagined that each rejection brought me closer to finding Teresa. So I continued down the streets, counting every fifth house. That first day, I made it inside only one house that reeked of urine. The old woman who answered the door and let me in was so overwhelmed by the children she was trying to care for that I excused myself after only a few minutes, though I could see that she was hungry for adult company.

I spent the rest of the week in this manner, knocking on doors of every type, climbing the stairs to dingy apartments to wander hallways, asking everyone, anyone, Did you know of a Teresa de la Landre, a painter, a professor husband, a child? By the time the weekend arrived I was tired from the walking and the heat that yet lingered; and perhaps my exhaustion deepened a growing despair—again to walk the streets of a Havana lovely and sordid, offering up every florid variation of decay, every version of destruction, like a patient with a spectacular disease from whom one cannot turn away. I visited only two houses on Saturday morning and spent the rest of the afternoon lying face up on the bed in my room at the Habana Libre, watching the clouds drift by through the open window. I had scaled back my note taking and found myself more and more peering into little alleyways, poking around in small open garages, searching for the yellowed photographs of strangers.

At some point I must have fallen asleep, and when I woke the window was dark. I got up with a start—there was something to do. And I remembered dinner at Caridad's. I wasn't even sure if I could find her house again. Frantically I searched my notes for an address, and found none. I showered and dressed quickly and ran out the door. I expected to first find the Pain de Paris and then remember from there. But as soon as I turned down a street, I heard someone calling my name and looked up to find a young man standing on a balcony, waving to me.

Again the door was opened as if by a ghost and I climbed the darkened steps up to Caridad's house. The dining room was brightly lit, and the smell of cooking returned to me the notion of home that years of travel had almost buried. The young man greeted me with a kiss on the cheek as if we were old friends. He was polite and funny and, I noted, very beautiful; and when he told me that his mother would be out in a short while I found myself at a loss for anything to say in return. He sat me down and disappeared into the kitchen, returning with two glasses and a bottle of French wine. My uncle brought a case of this last time he was here, he said, but neither my mother nor I much appreciate wine, so it has lasted us more than a year.

The wine was delicious, and a few moments later I found myself holding my glass out for more. Presently Caridad wheeled out, trailing a scent of lavender and so carefully made up that even her son smiled on seeing her. In his presence, Caridad seemed younger, lighter. Before long I found myself laughing with them and trading impressions of the city. I had the feeling—a common illusion, especially for the perpetual tourist—that I had known these two for a very long time.

After a while, Caridad announced that dinner was being served. The house had a formal dining room, which I had not seen on my first visit. And I was surprised, walking into it, to find a young black woman setting the table. She was dressed very well also, in a sleeveless silk green dress. She did not look up when we walked in, and after a while I realized that it wasn't because she was sullen, but because she was absorbed in her task. Each napkin had been expertly folded over the pale ivory plates. The glasses were lined up, the silverware polished. The others didn't address her, and after a while she disappeared into the kitchen. Caridad held her arm out toward a chair and told me to sit. I learned that the son, Manny, worked as a tour guide with the Nacional Hotel. He offered to give me a tour of El Vedado, since I seemed so interested in the neighborhood. It's one of Havana's newer areas, he said. The whole history of the city, Manny said, could be seen as a collective interest in outrunning the past, from the old center to La Vibora to El Vedado and on to the suburban dream of Miramar. As he talked I watched from a corner of my eye as the black woman brought out plate after plate of food and placed them on the linen runner in the center of the table. White rice, black beans, a wide basin of shrimp, potato salad, a plate of lobster tails in butter and parsley, a plate of stewed chicken. I sat back in my chair, now completely absorbed by the food and not listening to a word of the conversation. The woman brought out two more dishes filled with salad, and after arranging it all and bowing slightly, she sat down next to me at the table, raised a toast to Our Guest and we all clinked glasses. I waited for someone to make the introductions, and when no one did I introduced myself to the woman, whom I now had decided was not hired help but part of the family. The woman nodded, took my hand and resumed eating without saying a word. Neither Caridad nor her son ever directed conversation her way. This curious situation intrigued me, and I waited all evening to ask about it, but never found the right moment.

After dinner, the black woman stood, picked up everyone's dishes and disappeared into the kitchen. Then she came back for the platters of food, many of which, of course, were still more than half full. After a short time, she returned from the kitchen with a plate of flan and a small pot of fruit preserves from England, all of which she set on the table. As we ate dessert, Caridad told me that she had been in a wheelchair since 1985 and that doctors had never been able to explain why she had suddenly lost feeling in her legs. I had been very ill for some days with a terrible fever, she said. Gradually I thought that I was beginning to lose a sense of my body. As if I were floating. The doctors said it was a common effect of the medicine. But when I finally got better I discovered that I could no longer move my legs.

She looked over at her son before continuing. So I live up here, above the ground, suspended, floating again. I have friends to call in an emergency. Once, a delivery boy forgot, despite my many reminders, to close the door behind him on his way out. The system that Manny set up, you see, doesn't work for closing the door, only opening it. I hurried to the balcony and shouted out after him, but he didn't hear, or he refused to hear. So I called up one of my friends and she came and shut the door. Once a month, Caridad continued, Manny carries me and my wheelchair down and we go to La Coppelia. After, he'll take me on a little tour of the neighborhood, just to remind me. I'll see all the old places; each month, it seems, a new store has gone up or another building has crumbled. I think for Manny it's enjoyable. But I can never stay down there for long, Caridad said: the crush of people, the smell of exhaust, the cars so close and menacing . . . . No, I've come to prefer the world from up here.

She was quiet for a while, and we finished our desserts in silence. No one had yet spoken to the black woman so I turned to her and asked if she also lived in the neighborhood. She traded glances with Caridad and smiled at me before getting up with the dessert dishes and disappearing into the kitchen. I never saw her again.

I followed Caridad and Manny to the living room, where we took our coffee and I told them more of Teresa's story. My talk of the past caused Caridad to reminisce a little about what she called "those times"—aquellos tiempos, and I was reminded that nostalgia is not the exclusive province of exiles; or perhaps that one can be an exile without ever having left, can be an exile, so to speak, from time.

I told Caridad that a friend of mine in Miami had mentioned El Gato Tuerto and I asked her if it was still around. Caridad sat a long time with her eyes closed, then said: It was in El Gato Tuerto—this was the end of the 1950s, the beginning of the 1960s—where Miriam Acevedo would present herself, dressed all in black. Later, in the seventies, when I could still walk there on my own, I would go to hear Portillo de la Luz, Elena Burke. Caridad opened her eyes and looked at me. These names don't mean anything to you, she said. How strange that is. . . . Over the years, Caridad continued after a while, the place came to the point of collapse. Manny here tells me that it's been remodeled. But I doubt it's the same, she said.

If I were you, I wouldn't even bother going there. With this, she turned to her son and asked him to bring her a photo album from the dresser in her bedroom.

He returned with not just the album, but a plastic bag full of black-and-white photos. My heart did a little leap. Caridad reached into the bag and after a moment pulled out a photo of a lovely young woman dressed in a black stole and a long sequined dress. She sat for a while looking at it and then passed it to me without comment. We spent the next hour or so like this until the shadow that had been lingering over Caridad's face finally obscured it altogether and she gathered her photos and abruptly wheeled herself back to her bedroom, calling after Manny to help her get ready for bed. I stood quickly and hastened to say my good-byes, but Manny put a hand to my shoulder and asked me to sit for a bit. This I did, and after a while Manny returned, shutting the door to his mother's room behind him. He went to the dark armoire and pulled out a bottle of brandy and filled two small glasses, one of which he handed to me. She gets like that, he said. It is not about anyone or anything. He took a sip of brandy and then said, Come—I want to show you something. He led me into a small room off the dining room with a couch and a small table and, to my shock, a wide-screen television set hooked up to a satellite dish. The satellite dish was inside the room, pointed out at a high window. It's illegal to have it, he said, following my gaze; that's why it's inside. Manny smiled and turned on the set. We get about two hundred channels, I think, though I've never counted, he said. You are really crazy about sports in the U.S., aren't you? I've

never seen so many channels for sports. We get everything—
French movies, Italian game shows. But you know what it is my
friends always want to watch when they come up here? I raised
my eyebrows in a question. He sat on the couch and hit the remote control. CNN, he said and laughed.

I sat with Manny deep into the night, watching first CNN
and then a broadcast of *La Dolce Vita*. My head drifted onto
his shoulder, and I must have slept. It was nearly morning
when I woke. He had turned off the television and was sleeping also. I had a moment of small panic, and then I sat apart
from him very carefully. Now that he slept I could look on
him more closely—the dark curly hair, the fine cheekbones,
the full dark lips. I wanted so much for something to stir in
me, to feel something of the transcendence that Teresa had
described. But once again it eluded me. Instead I was overcome by the night, the flat walls, the shabbiness that seemed
ready to break free—in spite of Caridad's valiant efforts—
from every corner. I kissed Manny lightly on the forehead
and quietly let myself out, making sure to pull the door shut
behind me when I reached the bottom of the stairs.

For the next few days I avoided Caridad's immediate neighborhood, concentrating instead on the streets to the west and
north. Finally, I decided to send a cake from Pain de Paris up
to their house by way of thanks. I never saw them again.

Three days before I was set to leave, I had come no closer
to finding Teresa. I'd been foolish to believe that I would be

able to accomplish in one trip what I had not been able to accomplish in almost ten years of visits.

Near the end of the week I awoke early and realized that I could not bear another conversation with strangers. The tendency of the Cuban to talk about everything but the subject at hand had worn me down to the size of a pencil stub. I'd come to see it as a kind of aggression, a particular type of aggression perhaps indigenous to people who felt they had no other weapon at their disposal but the power to drive someone slowly mad through endless soliloquies, performed with aggrieved tones and an upraised, scolding finger.

Remembering the printmaking studio that Ileana had told me about, I took a taxi to the cathedral. I had no trouble finding the studio, which stood at the end of a narrow alley. I stepped inside without anyone stopping me or asking if I needed anything and spent the better part of an hour wandering around the vast room alone.

Finally a man approached and, recognizing his name, I told him Ileana had sent me. The man who ran the place—I made the mistake of calling him the owner, and he laughed—led me to his office on the top floor. I asked him if he had anything by an artist named Teresa de la Landre. He pursed his lips and thought for a while. No, he said. I don't think I've ever heard of that name. Is she a young artist? No, I said, from the fifties. I'm sorry, my love, we really don't have much here from that time. He smiled. The artists we have now—he opened his hands— are from a different era. I laughed, and suddenly afraid that I had been impolite, I asked if he would mind giving me a little tour of the vast gallery. I ended up buying two pieces, one by Bonachea and another by Jose Omar, which now hang in my house.

I returned by taxi to the hotel with my paintings. It was already late, and the evening crowds were gathering: the young scruffy backpackers from Germany, the oily old Spanish men, the beautiful prostitutes. I paid the driver, and he put his hands to his chest and said, Where are you going tomorrow, I will come and wait for you. I will wait for you my entire life. Charmed and perhaps a bit intoxicated by the slow work of the city on my senses, I kissed him lightly on the cheek. I gathered my things and made my way to the entrance. But before I arrived there, a young woman stepped in front of me. I had once before been propositioned in this way, and I turned my face away and continued walking until she whispered, Are you the woman who has been looking for Teresa de la Landre? I stopped, my hands suddenly trembling on the paintings. Who are you? I asked. Come with me, she said. I hesitated. Every trip to Havana is a dance between wanting to believe in the good of people and protecting oneself from the desperation that poisons every interaction. After a moment's considering, I said, No, you come with me. I motioned for her to follow me through the glass doors of the hotel. The porter who opened the door for me hesitated and then made eye contact with a security guard inside. The man rushed over and very politely asked me in Spanish if we were staying in the hotel. In English, I told him that in fact we were. The man let us through. I sat with the woman at the lobby bar and ordered two mojitos for us.

The short confrontation with the security guard had given me new confidence, and, quite able to hide my shaking, I asked the young woman what it was she really wanted.

I am the daughter, she said, of a woman who used to work for a woman who I think is the one you are looking for.

I remained impassive. Yes? I said.

You've been asking for a Beatrice, she said. But my mother's name is Matilde. And you've been looking for a Teresa de la Landre, but my mother worked for a woman named de la Cueva. Still, she said, I think she is the woman you are looking for.

What makes you think so?

The woman reached into her purse and pulled out a rumpled sheet of paper. She handed it to me. De la Cueva gave this to my mother some years back, she said.

I took the paper and unfolded it. Neruda's poem had been carefully handwritten, and though it was faded in parts I thought—or maybe I wanted to think—the writing seemed familiar.

I raised my eyebrows. I've mentioned the poem to several people, I said, trying to keep my voice even and steady. It's not so hard to reproduce.

The young woman had grown more and more fragile the more confident I became, and it wasn't long before I began to feel some pangs of guilt. Still, I was not going to be taken for a fool. The unlikely coincidence was not lost on me. For years I had visited the country, walking the streets far more assiduously than I had this time, and nothing had come of it. Why now? What were the chances? In the intervening years, the world had not changed very much, but Havana had. People were desperate in a way they had never been. Might not they be tempted to construct an elaborate lie? I cursed myself for having been so promiscuous with my information, for once again failing to note every detail of my interactions.

The woman in front of me seemed smaller and paler with every passing second. And I was caught inside conflicting thoughts and emotions. I leaned back and was silent.

I think my mother could help you, the woman said. What harm is there in trying? What harm is there in trusting?

I spent the following morning making arrangements to return to Miami. I had decided to leave a day earlier than I'd originally planned, but changing the date proved to be difficult. Frustrated and angry and tired, and once again disillusioned by this city, I collapsed into bed by mid-morning. I turned on the television and flipped channels. Finally, running out of distractions, I reached into my pocket and fingered the paper where the young woman had written down her mother's address.

That afternoon, after lunch in the hotel, I took a taxi downtown. The driver was a disagreeable old man who kept insisting on taking me to the French restaurant for lunch. There you will eat very well, he insisted. The downtown area, it is all for tourists only, no Cubans there. After a few minutes of this, I finally lost my temper and screamed at the driver to do what he was told. This outburst, so unusual for me, I instantly regretted, especially because the disagreeable old man had managed to transform himself into a wounded creature whose eyes now and then darted in fear and sympathy to the rearview mirror. When he finally deposited me at the address I had given him, I tipped him almost 50 percent of the amount. He took the money with the same wounded expression and drove off without saying a word.

I found myself in the middle of a street so narrow that I thought it might be an alley, and instantly I feared that the odious driver had dumped me in some crime-infested corner of the city as punishment for my American imperiousness.

Just as I was about to walk in the direction of the sea-smell, I was stopped by a very old woman. She was brown and wrinkled and bent over, and I would have missed her entirely had it not been for her tugging on my skirt.

You are the one looking for Teresa de la Cueva?

Teresa de la Landre.

Yes, that is what she chose to call herself for you. She didn't want you to come looking for her.

Where is she? I said.

The old woman regarded me very closely, and I was reminded of Dr. Caraballo's intense scrutiny of my face. After a moment she said, Yes, of course.

Where is she? I repeated.

The old woman pointed up to a window in a dilapidated old building. This is where she worked. Maybe she told you something of her studio.

Is she up there? I asked.

The old woman smiled. Of course, she said. She is up there.

With labored steps, the old woman began to walk to the building. But I stayed in the street. I had come this far; I had spent two weeks in the new Havana without anyone's trying to pull a knife on me, without falling prey to any scam except for the dinner with Judi. Now what? What if I climbed the stairs after this fragile old lady, perfectly chosen for her fragility, beyond suspicion? What if upstairs a gang of toughs awaited? The old woman turned at the door. I stood in the middle of the street. The old woman watched me.

Trust me, she said. I have no reason to lie to you.

In fact, if someone had wanted to rob me, they could have done it right where I stood, the street was so quiet and deserted. And what if my mother. . . . My God—my mother; to say the words alone . . . What if my mother were upstairs waiting for me? But why hadn't she come down? Was she in a wheelchair? Was she in fact Caridad? My mind was a jumble of ideas, and I longed to run away from myself, from my insecurities and my cautions.

Finally, scarcely aware of my movements—when I think back on that day it was as if I had been half paralyzed by my longings—I took one step and then another until I reached the door where the old woman stood. Then together we climbed the flight of stairs. This time I had to wait for my companion, and the climb seemed endless. We turned one corner and then another and walked down dark hallways full of cooking smells until we stood before a door. The old woman fumbled with a key, but the door wouldn't open. She went through a few other keys in her collection; still the door was shut tight. Finally, she knocked ever so lightly. There was silence, and then the sound of faint footsteps on the other side. My heart rose. The door opened, and the woman who had met me at the hotel the previous night stood before us. In her arms, she held a big package wrapped in white paper. She smiled without saying anything and then squeezed past us and was gone.

The old woman asked me to follow her inside.

The apartment was just a single room with a toilet, visible through a tattered curtain, in one corner. A hot plate had been set up on a pair of boxes. And all along the walls were leaned up painting after painting. The old woman was talking to me, but I didn't hear what she said. Slowly I began to walk along the walls. The paintings were sometimes piled three and four deep, and many canvases had begun to peel away from their frames. I looked back at the woman, and she nodded. I crouched down to the paintings and began to carefully sift through them. Some still lifes, an orange, cubes of color layered one on the other. Near a corner, I stopped at a painting marked "From My Window," and when I pulled it forward, I saw that it was part of a series. The first was a daytime view from a window into a courtyard, done mostly in whites and grays except for a red window frame in the far left corner. The second was an afternoon view: dark shadow slanting across the bleached-out buildings. Then the same view in the blue of early night, the red window frame now a darker smudge. The last painting was entirely black except for the reflection of a lightbulb on the window and the dark buildings beyond. I looked at this last painting for a long time before I caught, in the far right corner, the small image of a woman, her face turned slightly, her features blurred in the clouded mirror of the glass. Barely breathing, I moved in closer, but then the face lost all definition and all I could make out were the tiny strokes of color. I stood and looked from the painting to the old woman.

Where is she? I said, and my voice was almost a whisper.

The old woman stood by me for a while in silence, and then she walked over to the worn couch and sat down. She patted the seat next to her. The couch faced the apartment's one window, and when I sat on it, I recognized the view from the paintings. Is that her face? I asked. Where is she? The old woman was quiet. I looked around the apartment. Mold crawled up the walls. The ceiling, mottled here and there by water stains, had peeled away in parts, exposing the wood beams. The place had a feeling of sickness and death. And had it not been for the paintings, I would likely have fled, filled as I was now with a strange anxiety.

The old woman took my hand. She worked here for many years, she finally began.

Where is she?

The old woman continued, ignoring me. And even after her husband died, she kept this place. In the late seventies, it became harder and harder to obtain materials. Most of her friends had left for Miami. She used to tell me that she worked not for the paintings themselves but for the smell of the oils, which took her back to happier times. She worked until she could no longer get her oils, and she switched to charcoal. But then paper became scarce. I watched your mother, unable to paint, go mad before my eyes.

The old woman stopped at the mention of my mother and looked at me for a while before continuing.

They had come for her husband, after the Bay of Pigs. That's when they were rounding up everyone.

He was arrested?

The old woman pursed her lips and nodded slightly.

I don't understand, I said. She told me he was traveling in Spain.

She told you this? When? In her letters?

She said he was in Spain when I was born.

The old woman looked at me for a while. And then shrugged. I don't know, she said. If she told you that . . . I don't know why . . . She was quiet for a while. And then she began again, What I understood was that Carlos had written something—I don't know.

Calixto?

Carlos. Calixto, he used both names. The woman continued, Something in a Spanish journal that got back to the authorities. Your mother took it very hard. After that, she would walk to her studio, to this apartment, every morning, work for a few hours and return home in the afternoon. Some days she was fine. Others, she was in her own world, talking to duendes, seeing ghosts.

The old woman was quiet then. She leaned back on the couch and closed her eyes. She kept them closed for such a long time that I thought she had fallen asleep.

My fingertips were cold inspite of the heat.

Who was my father? I asked

The woman remained still, eyes closed. Why would you ask that?

Did my mother know Che Guevara?

The woman opened her eyes and turned to me.

I looked around the room. Did he come up here? In this room? Didn't she paint him? Where are all the drawings of him? I know she made drawings of him.

The woman rose from the couch with some difficulty and walked to the window.

After a while she said, Your mother loved Che very much, yes, as we all did. But only from a distance. The old woman turned to me, and she was dark against the light coming in from the window. Many people loved him, men and women. Many people. But your mother never knew him. She would have told me. You must understand this.

The woman stepped away from the window. She poured water into a tin pot and set it over the hot plate. When it boiled, she stirred in the coffee. She returned with two grimy cups.

When she handed me my coffee, I noticed a spot of blue paint beneath her fingernails. She followed my eyes, but didn't say anything.

When things became very difficult, the old woman continued, Teresa had to give up her house. There is no sale of property here, as you know. She smiled. But in those years everything was for sale. I don't know who lives there now. My daughter goes to that neighborhood now and then. I've never been back.

I drank my coffee. Sounds came through the walls: a baby crying, a man coughing, faint singing.

These were difficult times for most of us, the woman continued. But your mother—she lived in her imagined country, this promised garden of ours. She wouldn't hear of shortages or hardships. She woke in the morning, rolled up her mattress and began painting. I used to envy her. Always it was left to me and my daughter to find what we could to eat. The old woman said this without bitterness. But her voice had grown softer.

Where is she now? I asked.

The woman didn't answer. She picked up my cup and rinsed it in the bathroom sink.

When she returned, I asked, Are you Teresa?

The woman smiled and looked at her hands. I paint now and then; I try to. Your mother had made friends with a Spanish couple who came every year, and they brought her acrylics. She left behind three boxes of them.

Left behind, I said.

The old woman was very quiet before continuing.

About a year ago, she said, Teresa set to work, sometimes for hours, on some writings. I asked her many times what it was she was writing, and I tried to look into her books now and then. But she would get very angry with me. I realize now that she was writing this letter, or these letters, to you. It took her many months to finish them. I don't know how she got them to you, she didn't speak of it to me, but I suppose her Spanish friends took care of it.

In those months that she was writing, the woman continued, I had detected some of her old sadness. But I was absorbed in my own problems. We were three of us living in this little room. I wanted my daughter to do something, be someone honorable. The pressure now to have money . . . you can imagine what it is. At best they become waitresses in a jazz club. At worst . . . you've seen. How do you tell these young people that it's in their interest to study? What good is a degree? Learning for learning's sake, this is a fine idea. But it does nothing for hunger.

Last December, the old woman continued, your mother climbed to the roof, as she often did. You can see the whole of the malecón from there and at the end, La Cabaña, like a ghost fortress. Often, she would spend hours out there, in good weather even taking a small notebook for sketching. I returned from shopping in the late afternoon; I remember it was already getting dark. As the years have gone on in this country, simple tasks take longer and longer. And when you don't have dollars . . . well.

Here the old woman looked at me for a long time and sighed before continuing. My daughter was out at a dance rehearsal. I was surprised to see the room dark. But I turned on the lights and went about preparing dinner. When my daughter came

home and Teresa still had not returned, I sent her up to the roof
to call her down for dinner. My daughter returned alone, saying Teresa was not up there. We waited a few more minutes and
then, too hungry to wait anymore, we sat down and ate. It was
unusual for Teresa to miss dinner. But not unprecedented. She
was still very beautiful. And now and then there were nights
when she didn't return and no one asked her any questions.

The old woman stopped and closed her eyes. After a moment, tears began to darken her lashes.

They found her body in the morning, the old woman said.
The police didn't bother to come for a report.

Why?

The woman took my hand.

I don't understand, I said.

I felt, in my chest, the first pull of mourning. This woman
who had put herself always beyond my grasp. Had her notes
really been a fiction? An elaborate fable of her own life and
death?

Why? I asked myself this question too, the woman said. It
is natural to feel responsible. I was sorry for myself, too. Sorry
that I hadn't done anything and now I had this terrible trag-
edy and I was all alone with it. And then as the days went on,
I began to cry and couldn't stop. Crying not just for her, but
for all the things I didn't tell her. Crying for this beautiful
woman so broken by hoping.

I looked away. Late afternoon was settling.

She talked about you. She wanted things to be right.

Was she sorry?

The old woman sighed and stood. Your mother was very committed to her work. And her ideas. In the late sixties, she abandoned her earlier subjects and began to paint portraits of El Che almost exclusively. She spent hours erasing and redrawing, layering colors. When I wasn't out trying to get food or standing in line for something, I sat here and watched her paint. Those were happy times, still. Though a sadness had fallen on her since his death, still there was something bright in her movements. Day after day, she painted.

The old woman looked at me. Yes, she said, you are right; she painted many pictures of him. She left behind dozens of portraits. Then she added: But most of them are gone.

She stopped. I didn't say anything.

We have to eat somehow, she said after a moment. Without dollars in this country there is nothing. You want to see my ration book? It's worthless. No one uses them anymore. I pay a boy to pick up the few items we can still get—a miserable handful of rice, some bread. It is not even worth going down to get it myself. What were we supposed to do?

The woman paused and sighed. She walked to the paintings. A few months ago, she said, my daughter began to take the paintings of El Che down to the plaza, where the booksellers gather. She sold the first one to a German man for fifty dollars. Can you imagine? Fifty dollars—a fortune. And she said the man didn't even hesitate, just picked out the money from his wallet as if he'd been paying for a piece of candy. So the next time, my daughter went down with a painting and asked for one hundred dollars. This too sold. She sells them now for two hundred, and the tourists buy them.

The woman lifted her feet, and I noticed for the first time a new pair of Nike running shoes. She smiled. But mostly, she said, the money goes for food. And we're saving. Who knows what will come.

The woman had been talking more excitedly than she had all afternoon, but suddenly she stopped. If you would like to take one of these paintings, of course . . . you are welcome. She began to walk up and down, pointing at this painting and that.

Did she ever make any of herself?

The woman shook her head. And then she walked to the series of the window. She took the last one and held it out for me. Yes, that is her reflected there in the corner, she said. But as you can see for yourself, it is a difficult likeness.

I took the painting from her.

Are there any left of Che?

I stood looking at her.

Very few, she said. After a moment, she added, We still have some rough studies she did, pencil and charcoal.

She opened a cabinet and began going through the papers inside. I sat on the couch again with the blurry self-portrait of my mother. I couldn't even tell what color her hair was. I moved it back and forth, trying to find the angle and distance that made her face appear most clearly.

After a few moments, the woman sat beside me on the couch. She unrolled a length of white paper and handed it to me.

As I left, I pressed some money into her hands. She closed her eyes and lowered her head.

I flew back to Miami on a Sunday night. The pilot circled and circled above the city, an ominous silence from the cockpit. Below, the city lights shone up from the gloom. All around, dark clouds obscured the evening sky. The descent went badly, and several people became ill. When the plane finally touched down, it did so with such force that the overhead bins popped open, spilling suitcases and jackets into the aisles and contributing to a few anxious screams, followed, when the plane finally began to taxi, by relieved applause.

The city, I learned, was in one of its periodic grips of hurricane fever; here and there homes and storefronts had been boarded up. I decided to skip the supermarket and make do with whatever I had in my freezer. That night, I listened to the wind outside and thought of Teresa; and for a brief moment just before I closed my eyes, I too believed that weather might roil the inner landscape.

The storm passed in a few days, leaving behind only the shredded clouds of a mild tropical depression. In the weeks that followed, I underwent a period of the most profound exhaustion I had ever experienced. For some days I was unable to work. I lay in bed day after day. What gripped me wasn't sadness in the way that one usually understands it, I could not even experience anything close to despair. I simply felt very tired. It was as if the world about me were in the grips of a terrible illness and now lay next to me, softly exhaling a stale breath. The song of the mockingbirds at my window now failed to stir me; the cloud shadows did nothing to me. I simply lay, as I imagined an animal or an insect might, wanting nothing, dreaming nothing, not content or discontent, just caught in a sort of waiting.

As I have few intimates, my condition went largely unnoticed. And then as the weeks and then months passed, I noticed that I was gradually improving, that the sunlight felt warm again, that leaves silvered with rain could be beautiful.

When finally I emerged, it was the middle of autumn and the days had softened. I decided to take a trip out west. But at the last minute I canceled my flight and instead drove up to Sebastian Inlet, where all those years before I had begun my life of travel.

Sitting on the beach, I made plans for another trip to Cuba. It would be an official one, and I would try to look up my birth certificate. Maybe talk to people in the government. It seemed very simple and logical, and I didn't know why I hadn't planned on it before. But when I returned to Miami, I found that I kept putting off the plans. I made appointments to see Ileana and Dr. Caraballo and then canceled them. Each time I thought of pursuing the truth of the story, I felt a bit of the creeping exhaustion that I had only just escaped. I decided then to think no more of Teresa, and put away her papers. I wrapped up the charcoal drawing of Che and hid it behind the winter clothes. A year after that last trip to Cuba, I came under contract with the telephone company, and by concentrating all my energies on writing corporate reports and small company articles, I hoped to forget the strange packet of memories my mother had bequeathed to me.

* * *

And yet, once an idea grips you, even the physical world will conspire to hold you fast to it. So it is when every object— every green branch, every cloud shadow—recalls to us a beloved. And so it was with me and Teresa's story and the memory of the man she had loved.

A recent winter, browsing in Manhattan, I entered a bookstore to escape the cold. I made my purchases and was ready to walk out when a box of holiday cards made me stop. *Vive la Christmas!* they said. And there again, against an olive-drab background, was the familiar face, the curled dark hair, the steady gaze, and above the serene eyes, a red and white Santa hat, accented with a comandante's star.

I found as the weeks passed that I could not escape his face. Once I looked up at a giant billboard and met his eyes in an advertisement for a clothing store. Another time I turned my car around at a light so I could follow a man in a red convertible that I was sure was him. I found myself staring one day at a little boy in the mall who looked so much like the small Che in a photograph that I had cut out of a book that I drew an angry comment from the woman I took to be the boy's mother. When I willed myself to stop examining people's faces for traces of him, I began to recognize him in the graceful arc of a palm, in a stone face set high on a wall.

As I began to see him in unlikelier and unlikelier places, I came to believe that in a secret way he was seeking me out; I began to wonder if the dead, too, have memory.

* * *

Some months ago, I found myself in Paris, on contract to write about the future, or lack of it, of fiber-optic technology.

The day before my flight back to the States, I wandered into a neighborhood where the woman at my small hotel had assured me I would be able to find the most interesting antique stores. I strolled from store to store, walking amid polished desks and gilded lamps and doing my best to be polite. I spent a few hours roaming the stores. But though they were clean and peaceful, I emerged from the last one disappointed. The stores were all organized on the grand, elegant scale of the city, each of them orderly and fresh-smelling, and not one with anything that would remotely interest me. I was about to give up and return to the hotel, for I was getting hungry and had yet to pack up my things for the early flight back, when I decided to turn down a narrow street. The decision was quite arbitrary, for the street looked like a quiet one of the sort that, in Europe, hold little more than private doors into private homes. But the sun that shone from the bottom of the street had caught the cobblestones and given them such beauty that it seemed ungracious to walk away.

I walked for a while, almost able to ignore the creeping anxiety that always marred the last day of a trip. Near the bottom, where the street turned onto a broader avenue, I came across a little storefront whose window, piled as it was with brown books and yellow paper, appeared to be in such a state of disorder and neglect that I was immediately intrigued. The store was dark, though, and I stood some time before the door wondering if it was closed. After a moment, I decided to give the door a little

push, and to my surprise it opened. Once my eyes adjusted, I noticed an older man sitting at a desk in the back. I nodded to him.
The store was a bit shabbier than the rest, and I was delighted to
find, behind a large desk, two cardboard boxes of old calendars
and record covers and black-and-white photographs. I must have
been in the store for about an hour when the old man rose—I
heard the scratch of his chair in the empty store—and stood beside me. He watched me look through the photographs for a
while and then said that if it was photographs I wanted to see,
he had another box to show me. And he opened a drawer and
pulled out several bunches of loose photographs, which he then
began to arrange, in a slightly overlapping pattern, on the old
desktop. Most of the photographs, judging from the style of dress
and hair, seemed to date from the 1950s, but then he pulled out
another group that seemed older, dating back into the twen-
ties, until he was spreading out browned photographs, almost
now completely faded, of women in elaborate dresses and hats
that seemed so far removed from our time as to make me wonder about the unbroken link to the past that I had always
assumed.

I went through the photographs in silence: the somber
faces of men, the round cheeks of children, the haughty stare
of a merchant, the curl in a pretty girl's hair. The man stood
by me and after a moment he said, Photographers labor dili-
gently with their lights and their chemicals, without realizing
they are agents of death.

When I turned to him he said, Roland Barthes—he is a
French writer. He was correct, the man said after a moment.

In our time, death more and more appears to reside most comfortably in the photograph. I stared at him, unsure of what to say. He shrugged, as if suddenly embarrassed. Look here, he said, beckoning me with his finger. I have a very old photograph here.

I followed him to his desk, where he turned on the overhead lamp and unlocked a nearby cabinet. He pulled out a glass case and held it with a shaky hand. It was a view of a garden, taken, it seemed, from a balcony through some buildings. This is the world's oldest photograph, he said. When I raised my eyebrows he added, Well, not this one, of course; this is a reproduction, about twenty years old. The original is in Texas now. They are restoring it. It is called, I believe, *The View from the Window at Le Gras.* The original was taken in 1826 by a country gentleman named Joseph Nicéphore Niépce. He used a camera obscura, a well-known novelty at the time, modified with a pewter plate that he coated with a kind of petroleum.

The old man looked at the photograph and then back at me. Amazing, yes? One wonders what he thought when he washed the plate and saw what he had made. This Niépce, you know, he was supposed to be something of a frustrated artist. He must have been delighted to be able to create something with his brains. The old man pointed to his head and laughed. You know, he wasn't able to interest the Royal Society in his new invention. But the little plate created some interest, and it was exhibited until 1898. After that, the old man continued, the plate fell into the peculiar obscurity of things we haven't yet learned to name, languishing beneath old papers, hidden among diaries and pressed flowers. Then, in 1952, after science had yielded to the world far more frightening imaginings, a historian became interested in the legend of the pewter plate and after much searching found the long-forgotten image.

The original photograph, though, the old man continued in a more somber tone, is almost completely faded. It must be viewed under special lighting, at a thirty-degree angle to the perpendicular, or else the landscape etched on the plate fades to nearly nothing.

I handed the frame back to the old man and thanked him, without realizing it, in Spanish. He raised his eyebrows. You are Spanish, then. I hesitated a moment before responding, No, Cuban.

Cuban! Ah, Cuba hermosa. My favorite country. Yes. Yes. Wait here.

He disappeared into a back room and emerged with yet another packet of photos. He flipped through them, and this time all the vistas were familiar: the royal palms flanking roads, a man on a tractor, the lush leaves coming through even in black and white. He must have noted the pleasure the photographs gave me, because he disappeared several more times to the back, each time emerging with another clutch of photos. We flipped through them all together. I was becoming conscious of the time and worrying about returning to my packing when one of the photos that he was turning onto the table caught my eye.

I held up my hand and dug through the pile again before finding it. I held it under the light.

I stood for some time holding this thin image in my hands. Already I was dreading the flight home: the sound of the engines beneath me, the liftoff, the sudden tearing weightlessness, the falling away of the earth.

And to come upon this photo now, so far from home. Surely I walked with ghosts. There he stands for all eternity, the young soldier with a yearning to record the world that lies before him, his hands light on the camera, his eyes searching ahead.

I handed the man my money and noticed that my hands were cold where they met his. After a moment, I said, For my mother. The man made a small bow with his head, but kept looking at me. Then he smiled to himself and nodded. He took my money, gave me my change and began to carefully wrap the photo, slipping it first into a plastic sleeve, then carefully sealing it shut before finally hiding it beneath layer on layer of brown paper.

Afternoon was ending by the time I returned to the hotel. I turned on the small light on the desk and stood at the window looking down into the street below. After a moment, I thought I heard a radio playing. Whether because of the conversation with the old man or because of the faint music now drifting through the walls, I thought for the first time in many months of my grandfather. I remembered the song that had been playing all those years ago when we had sat out on the porch together, *Still I see you in my dreams, and every sigh brings me back to you.* My grandfather with his silences and quiet gestures. How little I knew him, how lost the years now when I might have understood.

I stood by the window until the lights came on in the street below. I watched a couple walk along and stop under a street sign to kiss. Two boys ran past, throwing a ball between them. Then it was quiet. The street emptied. I turned from the window and back to the little room, now warm and yellow after the chilled blue of the street. Slowly, thinking of nothing, I began to pack my bag: my travel clothing, my books, a few pages of loose notes. And when I was done, I lay across the top the tightly wrapped photograph of a man standing alone with his camera, the future not yet a darkened plate; a beautiful stranger who, in a different dream, might have been the father of my heart.

NOTES

Though allusions to real people, living and dead, abound in the book, it remains a work a fiction. Teresa's story draws on the portraits of Ernesto Guevara in Jorge G. Castañeda's Compañero, *Jon Lee Anderson's* Che Guevara: A Revolutionary Life, *and Paco Ignacio Taibo II's* Ernesto Guevara También Conocido Como El Che. *Many of Guevara's quotes come from these works and his own writings. In addition, the author wishes to thank Ileana Oroza; Raúl Chibás; Gustavo Pérez Firmat; Dara Hyde; and her tireless agent Amy Williams and editor Elisabeth Schmitz, a magician if there ever was one. The author is especially grateful to her family in Miami: Saul, Maria, and Rose whose love is immeasurable; her family in Havana: Lourdes, Amarilys, Guillermo, and Laurita; uncle Dionisio Martínez, always the master of words; and her good friends Judy Battista and Anthony McCarron who have kept her well-fed and watered for many years. She is most indebted to her husband Dexter Filkins who, while covering the wars in Afghanistan and Iraq, still found time to read more versions of this story than anyone should be subjected to and read them more attentively than anyone would ever care to, and who very often managed to return with tattered and mud-stained manuscripts that kept all things in their proper perspective.*

Loving Che

Ana Menéndez

ABOUT THIS GUIDE

We hope that these discussion questions
will enhance your reading group's exploration
of Ana Menéndez's *Loving Che*. They are
meant to stimulate discussion, offer new viewpoints,
and enrich your enjoyment of the book.

More reading group guides and additional information, including summaries, author tours, and author sites, for
other fine Grove Press titles, may be found on
our Web site, www.groveatlantic.com.

QUESTIONS FOR DISCUSSION

1. Who is the hero of the novel? The narrator? Teresa, the other narrator? The eponymous Che? Is the concept of "hero" relevant to this book?

2. Do you think the book is a reliable window into Cuban politics, particularly the revolution? Teresa says that "it was the strange and dreadful excitement of a world turning, of everything staid and ordinary being swept away" (p. 50). What points of view, other than Teresa's, provide us with information about the Cuban revolution and its aftermath?

3. What other works of literature, art, or film have opened up Cuba for you? *Buena Vista Social Club*? Ana Menéndez's earlier book *In Cuba I Was a German Shepherd*? Do these works make you want to go to Cuba? How do these works make you feel about Cuba? Have they, in any way, changed your concept of that country?

4. Do you see a connection between Teresa recapturing Ernesto through her portrait of him and the narrator trying to retrieve her mother through memory and imagination?

5. Why did Teresa send her daughter away? Are her explanations on page 154 credible? "Someday I would give you a good life. Someday when my lover returned . . . I was waiting. How could I have been of help to you? Already, I read him in every move of your hands, smelled him on your sweet baby's breath. When you cried at night, I lay remembering the lost afternoons, how time had wrapped its eternity around us." Is it her passion for Che as well as for art that leaves her no space to be a mother? When Teresa speaks of a divided heart, she is referring to her married love as well as her adulterous love. Could her divided heart also describe her love of her child at the same time that she persists in rejecting her?

6. How do we decide what is truth in the book? The narrator's grandfather scorns her need for documented proof about her mother? Why? The book is filled with transitory lives and relationships, as though names were written in water. What are some of these shifting, disappearing names and relationships?

7. How does the narrator's being a nervous flier relate to her story? She explains that rummaging in junk stores for old magazines and faded photographs assuages her fears on the eve of a departure. Is this just fear of flying or is it larger existential angst?

8. What motivates the quest of the narrator? Is it the need to fill the void her mother left? Is it an odyssey she needs to provide purpose in her life? To become more truly Cuban?

9. What kind of person is the Che who emerges both in Teresa's memories and in the occasional, more objective observations? Did you like the device of photographs interspersed? Why or why not? Do you think all of us construct and revise our own histories through "scraps of memory" (p. 48)?

10. What are the consequences of loving someone bigger than life, someone whose "first desire is to wear furrows into the earth" (p. 113)? Che offers his own view: "No, he says, and his hands are already over my skin. No matter how much we try, we will always love some things more than others. And some things we will love so much that we will honor them until death" (p. 119). Is he speaking of love for a person? Or for an idea, a revolutionary ardor? Both?

11. How are exile and madness linked? See the early pages, and consider the results of passion, nostalgia, and obsession. Does exile need to be geographic? Or can it be internal disassociation? Think of Caridad and her sense of floating and inexplicable paralysis.

12. What are some clues, true or false, that make the reader wary about reality in the story? For instance, "Even after all these years, I remember everything with a supernatural precision, with a certainty that is not given to actual life" (p. 130). How has Menéndez created simultaneously a mystery or ghost story, a love story, and a tantalizing game with aesthetics?

13. Do you end by believing Teresa's story? Is it possible that the whole Che love story was an elaborate justification for rejecting her daughter? Again, her overriding need to be an artist? Could even her artist life have been a fabrication? There seems to be no outside evidence of

Teresa's art, according to Ileana. What, however, does she say on pages 168–169 that leaves the door open? What does the narrator seem to believe by page 215?

14. Do you feel the narrator becomes her mother in the end? As she begins to see Che in every bush and palm tree, she wonders if "he was seeking me out; I began to wonder if the dead, too, have memory" (p. 221).

15. What are some memorable images in Menéndez's writing? One example is "a black Chevrolet sequined with the reflection of street lamps" (p. 22). How would you describe her style? Does she use evocative imagery to foreshadow and propel plot and character development? For instance, "But even before all that, even before I knew him, that day in my studio, I could see the death that gently draped him" (p. 66). Can you find other examples?

SUGGESTIONS FOR FURTHER READING

Che Guevara: A Revolutionary Life by Jon Lee Anderson; *The African Dream: The Diaries of the Revolutionary War in the Congo* by Ernesto "Che" Guevara, translated from Spanish by Patrick Camiller; *Back on the Road: A Journey Through Latin America* by Ernesto "Che" Guevara, translated from Spanish by Patrick Camiller; *Five Decades: A Selection—Poems: 1925-1970* by Pablo Neruda, translated from Spanish by Ben Belitt; *Selected Poems* by Pablo Neruda, edited and translated from Spanish by Ben Belitt; *Old Rosa and the Brightest Star* by Reinaldo Arenas, translated from Spanish by Ann Tashi Slater and Andrew Hurley; *Leaving Tabasco* by Carmen Boullosa, translated from Spanish by Geoff Hargreaves; *Remember Me* by Trezza Azzopardi

ABOUT THE AUTHOR

Ana Menéndez is the daughter of Cuban exiles who fled to Los Angeles in the 1960s before settling in Miami in the 1980s. She worked as a journalist for six years, first at *The Miami Herald* where she covered Little Havana, and later with *The Orange County Register* in California. Menéndez is a graduate of NYU's creative writing program, where she was a *New York Times* fellow. *Loving Che* is her first novel and has been translated into eleven languages. Her story collection *In Cuba I Was a German Shepherd* has also been translated into eleven languages. She lives in Miami Beach.